Obsession

Obsession

Treasure Hernandez

www.urbanbooks.net

Urban Books, LLC
97 N18th Street
Wyandanch, NY 11798

ISBN 13: 978-1-60162-617-2
ISBN 10: 1-60162-617-7

First Mass Market Printing February 2015
First Trade Paperback Printing December 2012
Printed in the United States of America

10 9 8 7 6 5 4 3 2 1

Distributed by Kensington Publishing Corp.
Submit Wholesale Orders to:
Kensington Publishing Corp.
C/O Penguin Group (USA) Inc.
Attention: Order Processing
405 Murray Hill Parkway
East Rutherford, NJ 07073-2316
Phone: 1-800-526-0275
Fax: 1-800-227-9604

Tiffany stepped off the public bus and took hurried steps down the block. She looked down at her watch and sucked her teeth—already twenty minutes late. She just knew her, boyfriend, Blake was going to flip the fuck out. Tiffany hated that she had to rush home from work every night, but it was either rush home or fight, and Tiffany was tired of fighting for nothing.

She ignored the catcalls from local hustlers as she strolled through the hood and entered her projects. She stepped onto the elevator and repeatedly tapped on the CLOSE DOOR button as the door to the elevator finally closed. She stepped off the elevator and made her way down the narrow hallway until she reached her door, where she took a deep breath as she stuck her key inside the lock and opened the door. She stepped inside and immediately saw Blake sitting on the couch with his feet propped up on the coffee table and a blunt between his lips. The look on his face told Tiffany that he was pissed off, as usual.

"Where the fuck you been?" Blake asked, his eyes never leaving the TV as he spoke.

"I been at work." Tiffany hung up her jacket, just praying that tonight wasn't going to be one of those nights.

Blake arched his brow. "You got off work a hour ago," he said, the blunt dangling from his mouth.

"I know, baby, but the bus was running a little late."

"Again, right?" Blake huffed as he stood to his feet. "You think I'm stupid?" he asked, walking up on her.

"No, I don't think you stupid," she said quickly.

"Yes, you do," Blake said as he and Tiffany stood nose-to-nose.

Blake demanded that Tiffany come straight home from work ever since the last time he'd called himself surprising her, picking her up from work. Instead of surprising her, he wound up being the one surprised. He'd found her at the bus stop, smiling and giggling at every word some smooth-looking cat spoke. Blake just sat back and watched for a few seconds before interrupting the conversation. Ever since that day, Tiffany was forced to come straight home from work, no exceptions.

"How much money you made tonight?"

Tiffany reached down and removed the money she'd made from tips from her purse. "Eighty-seven dollars," she said, holding out the bills.

Blake snatched the money from her hands and thumbed through the bills. "That's it?" he asked, his face crumpled up.

"Baby, it was slow in the restaurant tonight," she said, bracing herself for the punch or slap that she knew was coming. "You know I wouldn't hold out on you—"

Blake's hand quickly shot out and wrapped around her throat. Tiffany screamed and struggled to pry his hand from around her throat. Then he slapped her really hard.

Blaw!

"Didn't I tell ya ass to come straight home?" he snarled.

He punched Tiffany in her face like she was a man. Her head violently jerked backward from the force of the blow, as she dropped to her knees and blood dotted the floor. "You giving another nigga my money?" he said loudly, gritting his teeth.

"No," Tiffany pleaded. "I would never do—"

Another punch to her face forced her head to jerk backward again.

Tiffany just balled up as Blake took all of his frustration and problems out on her. She knew this ass whipping was coming once she found out the bus was running a little late. This was nothing new to her—so she took it like a trooper.

After Blake got too tired to beat on her anymore, he grabbed a handful of her hair and dragged her like an animal throughout the house, until he reached the bedroom, where he tossed her up onto the bed and snatched off her work clothes, popping all the buttons in the process. He pulled out his already hard dick and spread her legs open.

"Wait. I'm not even wet!" Tiffany yelled, hoping he would feel sorry for her and just let her be for the night.

Blake spat on his fingers and roughly rubbed them in between her legs before forcing himself inside of her. He lay on top of her and pumped with force until he felt himself about to come. He then quickly hopped up on her chest and jerked his dick until he came on her face.

"Dirty bitch!" He smirked as he left the bedroom, headed back out to the living room.

Tiffany slowly slid off the bed and made her way to the bathroom. She looked in the mirror and wanted to cry. She grabbed the rag from the rack and wiped Blake's semen from her face as she just looked in the mirror and cried. The once pretty girl, who favored the actress Nia Long, looked in the mirror and didn't recognize the girl she saw in the mirror.

Tiffany quickly hopped into the hot shower. The pressure from the shower head massaged her body. She closed her eyes as she let the water run all over her body and she softly punched the wall. She knew if she didn't get away from Blake soon, he was going to wind up either killing her or hurting her really badly. Either way, she had to go. She was no longer in love with him, and she was definitely tired of him beating on her.

Tiffany stepped out of the shower and quickly got dressed. She figured the faster she went to sleep, the faster it would be time for her to go back to work the next day.

Blake looked at her like she was crazy when she tried to slide into the bed with him. "Fuck you think you doing?" he asked, looking her up and down.

"What?" Tiffany said with a confused look on her face. "I'm about to go to sleep."

"Hmmph." Blake sighed. "Bitch, you must be crazy if you think you sleeping in this bed with me. Better get yo' ass down and sleep on the floor," he said in a nasty tone.

Tiffany simply grabbed her pillow and a sheet and lay down on the floor. She was so tired of fighting and arguing. She just decided to keep her mouth shut and do as she was told. She silently cried herself to sleep as she lay on the floor.

The next morning, Tiffany woke up feeling like shit. Her body felt like she had been in a heavyweight fight, and her vagina was on fire. She got up and saw that Blake wasn't in the bed. She quickly searched the whole house.

A small smirk danced on Tiffany's lips when she discovered that Blake was nowhere in the house. She hopped into the shower. When she got out, she quickly got dressed and made herself something to eat. She ate a grilled cheese sandwich and did what she did every day—think about how she could get away from Blake.

She checked her purse and saw that Blake had emptied it out and taken all of her money. "Fuck!" she cursed loudly as she looked over at the clock on the wall. Since she didn't have any money, that meant she had to walk to work. Almost thirty blocks.

Tiffany stepped outside into the New York cold weather and zipped up her North Face jacket as she prepared for the long walk to work.

“The Grind Don’t Stop”

Quick wasn’t usually a big drinker, but today was his best friend-slash-mentor, Lucky’s, birthday, so it was only right that he drank with his crime partner. Quick wore a black hoodie with a black leather bubble vest on top of that. The two bobbed their heads to the sound of Young Jeezy that flowed through the small radio that rested over in the corner, on top of the milk crate. Quick and Lucky posted up in front of the building, their mentality “trap or die.”

“You heard from that nigga Turf yet?” Quick asked, looking up and down the block for potential customers and police.

“Nah, not yet,” Lucky replied. “He should be hitting us up within the next week or two. I hope he bless us with something nice.”

“He better.” Quick paused. “’Cause I’m about ready to go grab the strap and hit a bank,” he said seriously.

Quick and Lucky had been hustling for the past two years, and it just seemed like if it wasn't one thing, it was another that seemed to stop them from coming up. Recently, they had been copping their work from the city's top and most ruthless drug dealer, Turf. The word was, Turf had heard how much and how fast they were moving the product and wanted to speak with the two men. That was about two weeks ago. But Quick and Lucky were starting to get impatient.

"Just be patient," Lucky said as he watched a toothless fiend named Vanessa stroll up, switching what was left of her ass like she was still popping.

"Hey, baby. What's up?" Vanessa said, flashing her toothless smile as she held her hand out.

"What's good, V?" Lucky gave the woman dap, quickly looking over both shoulders. "What you need?"

"I need three fat ones," she said excitedly, already anticipating how good the product was going to be.

"Yo, go in the building," Lucky told her without even looking at her.

Once Vanessa went inside the building, Lucky waited for about seven minutes before he went inside the building after her and served her.

He counted out her money. "What the fuck is this?" he asked, his face screwed up. "This only twenty-six dollars."

"Come on, you know I'm good for it, Lucky," Vanessa said, patting Lucky on his back. "I promise, the next time I come to cop, I'ma come correct."

Lucky thought about cursing the fiend out, but the truth was, Vanessa was one of their most loyal customers, so he let her slide. "Don't let it happen again," he lightly scolded.

Quick was standing in front of the building, getting his sip on, when he saw some nobody walking up. He didn't really feel for the guy, but he spent money with him, so he was always respectful.

"What's good, my nigga?" Blake said, his hand extended.

Quick looked at Blake's hand for a few seconds before shaking it. "What's good, fam?"

"I need two ounces," Blake said with his hands in his pockets. "I been moving this weed like it ain't no tomorrow," he lied. He couldn't tell Quick he had just beat up his girlfriend and had taken her money to buy two ounces that he just planned on smoking.

"I got you," Quick said as he entered the building, where he saw Lucky coming out of the staircase. "I'll be right back," he said as he and

Blake hopped onto the elevator. “So what’s good? Everything been good?”

“Yeah. Just been out here trapping.” Blake pulled out his money and began counting it on the elevator.

“Chill. Put that away,” Quick told Blake, looking at him like he was crazy. Quick hated dealing with fake hustlers. He felt that they were just in the way. But as long as they weren’t stopping his flow, he let them rock.

The elevator came to a stop, and Quick stepped off and led the way down the hallway. He stopped in front of a door, pulled out a set of keys, and opened the door. “Wait right here,” he told Blake as he went the back.

In the back room there were drugs all over the place. Quick found a scale and quickly placed two ounces of weed inside two separate Ziploc bags, and he returned to the living room. “Here,” he said, tossing the two ounces on Blake’s lap.

Blake stuffed the ounces down into his drawers as he handed Quick the money. “Good looking.” Blake gave Quick a pound then made his exit.

Quick stayed in the stash house for about ten more minutes just to warm up before he headed back outside to join Lucky.

“What I miss?” Quick said when he returned back in front of the building.

"Looks like you came back right on time." Lucky motioned his head to the black Escalade that pulled up to the curb. He immediately recognized the two men Wolf and Major Pain, who emerged from the truck, and headed toward the front of the building.

Wolf and Major Pain were the two wildest and most violent goons that Turf had on his payroll. They were ignorant, paid, and just didn't give a fuck about nothing or nobody. Lucky and Quick had heard several stories about the work those two men had put in over the past few years.

"What's good?" Major Pain said, giving dap to both Lucky and Quick. "Fuck y'all doing out here in this freezing-ass weather?"

"You know the grind don't stop." Lucky blew into his hands. "For a second, we was starting to think that Turf had forgot about us."

"Nah," Wolf said, speaking for the first time. "Shit been a little crazy on our end. That's why Turf sent us down here to holla at y'all."

"So what's up?" Quick asked, already not liking the sound of things.

Major Pain looked at Quick and smiled. "Y'all know that old-school nigga Frank, right?"

"The nigga that supply the whole Lower East Side?" Lucky said, making sure they were talking about the same person.

"Yeah, him," Major Pain said. "Well, Turf wants him out of the picture, so we can take over and start supplying the Lower East Side."

"So why can't y'all do it?" Quick questioned with a raised brow.

"'Cause," Wolf said, getting up in Quick's face, "Turf want y'all to do it. That's why!"

Lucky tried to defuse the tension between the two men. "What's in it for us?"

"Y'all do this for Turf, and y'all earn a position on the team," Major Pain told him. "No more standing outside in the cold, nickle-and-dim-ing." He smiled. "Plus, the job pays ten thousand cash."

"Apiece?" Quick asked.

"No, just a flat ten thousand," Major Pain replied. "So what's it going to be, gentlemen?"

Lucky looked up and down the block before he replied, "Give us some time to think about—"

"We'll do it," Quick said, cutting Lucky off. He didn't know what Lucky was thinking, but he definitely could use the money.

Major Pain smiled again. "I like this nigga. Y'all have a week to take Frank out."

"How do we contact you once that's taken care of?" Quick asked.

Wolf looked at Quick like he was crazy. "Nigga, you don't contact us, we'll contact you!" he said in a nasty tone, and he and Major Pain headed back to the Escalade.

Lucky huffed as soon as the Escalade pulled off. “What the fuck was that back there? That’s just why I don’t be letting you drink with me,” he said, snatching the bottle of Cîroc Coconut from Quick’s hands. “We don’t know shit about how Frank moves.”

“Fuck how he move.” Quick shrugged. “All I know is I need that money. If you don’t want to take the job with me, I’ll just do it myself.”

The truth was, Quick, tired of nickle-and-dim-ing, saw the bigger picture. This was just the kind of comeup he needed, and he’d be damned if he was going to let an opportunity like this slip through his hands. “So are you in or not?”

Lucky sucked his teeth. “Nigga, you know I’m in.”

The two laughed.

“Besides, I’d feel bad if you got killed by yourself.”

“I’m tired of struggling,” Quick said out loud to nobody in particular.

At the age of twenty-five, Quick had already felt like he had been through hell and back. Sometimes, he felt like he was put on this earth to just struggle and then die. He was just happy that Turf was giving him the opportunity to come up. Quick didn't care if he died on the job 'cause, if he didn't come up with something soon, he was really planning on trying to rob a bank, so the Frank job didn't sound too bad to him.

Lucky interrupted Quick's thoughts as he draped his arm around his neck. "You thinking too much. We gon' be fine. Stop worrying so much," he added as the two headed to his hooptie. "Let's grab us some food."

Lucky pulled his hooptie up inside IHOP's parking lot and cut the engine off. "I'm hungrier than a muthafucka," he said as he and Quick entered the restaurant.

Seconds later, the two men were handed menus and led over to a booth by the window.

"Cheer up," Lucky said. "Damn! You about to make me depressed."

"I'm just tired of losing," Quick responded as he saw the waitress making her way to their table. "I'm ready to win."

"How y'all doing today?" Tiffany said politely. "Can I start off by getting y'all something to drink?"

"Yeah, let me get some orange juice," Lucky said, looking over the menu.

"I'll have the same," Quick said as he and Tiffany locked eyes for a second.

"Coming right up." Tiffany slightly smiled then disappeared through the double doors that led to the kitchen.

As the waitress walked off, Quick made sure to look at Tiffany's nice-sized ass poking out through her work pants.

"You better stop looking at the waitress like that before Kat pop up out of nowhere and whip yo' ass," Lucky said half-jokingly.

"Fuck Kat! She don't give a shit about nobody but herself." Quick waved Lucky off. "But let's get down to business. We got a week to get rid of Frank."

"This shit going to be harder than it sounds. You know that, right?" Lucky said, exhaling loudly.

Before he could say another word, the waitress reappeared at their table carrying their drinks.

"Here you go," Tiffany said, politely setting their drinks down on the table. She glanced over at Quick, then her eyes immediately went down to the floor. She wasn't used to looking men in the eye. The last time she did that, Blake had almost beat her half to death.

"Are y'all ready to order yet?"

"Yeah," Lucky said, still looking over the menu that sat in front of him. "Lemme get some waffles and sausages."

Tiffany wrote down Lucky's order then turned and looked at Quick, who favored the rapper Maino. "You ready to order?"

"Yeah," Quick replied. "I'll take the T-bone steak and some onion rings." He handed Tiffany back the menu.

"Not a problem. Coming right up." Tiffany smiled as she walked off and disappeared through the double doors again.

"Damn! You was all in shorty mouth," Lucky teased.

"Nah, I just wanted to make sure she got my order right," Quick lied. He was really checking out the bruises on her face, which she had tried to cover with makeup. Quickly changing the subject, he said, "So how do you think we should handle this Frank situation?"

"I say we just take two days and watch how he move, then come up with a game plan."

Quick nodded his head up and down. He knew once this job was done, the money would definitely come rolling in, especially since he and Lucky would be on a winning team.

Everybody on Turf's team was paid and drove luxury cars. Quick was just so tired of losing, he was willing to do almost anything to win.

"Sounds like a good idea to me," Quick said as he watched Tiffany stroll back over to their table carrying their food.

"You guys enjoy."

Tiffany smiled as she walked back in the direction from which she had just come. When she was at work, it was the only time she had any peace. There, she was all smiles, but as soon as it was almost time for her to go home, that pretty smile always seemed to fade away.

After the two men finished their dinner, Quick paid the bill and left the nice waitress a twenty-dollar tip.

"You hanging out tonight?" Lucky asked Quick as the two slid back inside the hooptie.

Quick shook his head. "Nah, I gotta get home."

"Oh yeah, I forgot, if you don't get home, Kat gon' kick that ass." Lucky laughed loudly as he pulled off.

Quick laughed, but he also knew what his friend was saying was true. Kat was Quick's off-and-on girlfriend for the past two years. Quick didn't even know why they were still together, especially since all the two did was fight all the time like cats and dogs.

Lucky pulled up in front of Quick's house and placed the car in park. "You sure you ready to go in right now?" He laughed.

"Yeah, I gotta go face the music." Quick gave Lucky a pound and slid out of the car. "I'll holla at you tomorrow," he yelled over his shoulder as he walked up to his apartment. He took a deep breath as he stuck his key inside the lock and opened the front door.

As soon as Quick closed the door behind him, Kat came storming out of the room.

"Where the fuck you been all night?" she asked, rolling her eyes and placing her hand on her hip.

"What you mean, where I was at?" Quick asked with his face crumpled up. "I was out doing what I do."

"Doing what you do?" Kat echoed. "And what's that? Playing house with ya other bitches?"

Quick sighed loudly as he tried his best to ignore her. He walked over to the kitchen and opened the refrigerator.

Kat roughly grabbed the back of his shirt. "Don't turn your back on me while I'm talking to you!"

"Bitch!" Quick snapped. His hands shot out, grabbing Kat's bra as he shoved her back up against the refrigerator. "Stop acting stupid all the time!" he huffed. "I been out tryin'a get this money like I do every day, and you know that."

Kat, wearing nothing but a gold thong with the matching bra, stood hemmed up against the refrigerator. "Take your muthafuckin' hands off of me right now!"

Quick let go of Kat's bra and headed to the bedroom. He knew as soon as he stepped through the door, it was going to be drama. He tried his hardest to prepare for it, but it was totally different when up close and in person. He entered the bedroom and removed his shirt.

"What you think you doing?" Kat asked, entering the room behind him.

"I'm about to go to sleep. I hate when you act like this."

"I'm sorry, baby," Kat said in her baby voice. "But I just be so jealous."

"For what?" Quick asked. "All I do is bust my ass tryin'a get this money up for us, and as soon as I come home every night, you swear I been with another bitch all night. I'm tired of this shit!"

"I'm sorry, baby. I swear it won't happen again," Kat promised, like she did every time she acted foolish. "You know I just be missing you."

"We about to be straight though," Quick told her. "I got this little plan, so in about two weeks, we going to be straight. But I can't have you on my back like this all the time."

"I'm sorry, baby. Is there anything I can do to make it up to you?" Kat said, looking into Quick's eyes as she unbuckled his belt and slid his jeans down.

Quick didn't really want to have sex with Kat, but he couldn't turn down head or sex from Kat, which were both on point to the max.

Kat slid down to her knees as she took Quick into her mouth slowly. She lubricated his dick with her saliva as she began jerking it and sucking on it at the same time, going faster and faster. She hummed and moaned loudly as she performed.

After about ten minutes of sucking, she climbed on top of the bed on all fours and looked back at Quick, motioning with her finger for him to follow her.

Quick climbed onto the bed and entered Kat from behind. Kat moaned when she felt him enter her walls. With each stroke he delivered, she made sure to throw it back as hard as she could.

After twenty minutes of hard sex, Quick finally pulled out and exploded all over Kat's ass. "Damn!" Quick exhaled as he lay butt naked on the bed.

Kat quickly went to the bathroom to clean herself off. She was returning from the bathroom carrying a washrag to clean Quick up, when she heard his cell phone ring.

Kat's smile quickly turned into a frown. "Damn! You just got in the fuckin' house!" she huffed. "Why you ain't answering your phone? It must be one of your bitches!" Kat tossed the wet rag at Quick's face.

Quick moved the rag from his face and answered his phone. He spoke briefly then hung it up. Then he began to get dressed.

"Where the fuck you think you going?" she asked, folding her arms across her chest. "So what? Your next bitch call, and you jump up running?"

"Fuck is you talking about?" Quick said in an aggravated tone. "I have to go make a run real quick."

Kat sucked her teeth. "You must think I'm a fool."

Quick was getting ready to snap, but he held it together as he put his hoodie back on, followed by his vest. He grabbed a few ounces of weed then headed for the door.

"Quick, if you walk out that door, I swear, you better not come back." Kat was sick of being stuck in the house all the time by herself, and she was definitely sick of Quick and his lies.

"I'll be right back," Quick yelled over his shoulder.

"Well, you better take yo' shit with you, and I'm not playing, either," Kat said, anger all in her tone and body language.

Quick just shook his head as he exited the apartment. He didn't care what Kat said. He was going to get that money.

After Quick made the drop-off, he headed back to his apartment, only to find all his shit sprawled all over the front stoop. He quickly searched through the bags until he found his weed stash. He quickly stuck the seven pounds of weed inside a duffel bag and left all the other items right there on the stoop. He tossed the duffel bag onto the backseat of his own hooptie, deciding he might as well start tailing Frank a little sooner than he'd planned.

“Being A Fool”

Tiffany looked down at her watch as she stepped off the bus. She only had five minutes to be home. After what happened the other night, she definitely wasn’t trying to be late; so she began to jog home. She felt dumb as hell, jogging home, but it was either jog or get her ass beat, and she was tired of getting her ass beat. So jogging it was.

She reached the lobby and caught her breath while she waited for the elevator, her lungs about to explode out of her chest. She hopped onto the elevator, pressed her floor, then glanced down at her watch. She had made it home on time, with two minutes to spare. She hopped off the elevator and saw some light-skin chick, with a long weave and bamboo earrings, exiting her apartment.

“Girl, hold that elevator,” the light-skin girl said as she rushed to catch the elevator before the doors closed.

Tiffany looked at the light-skin girl running past her, but she had to make sure she wasn't seeing things. She continued on down the hallway until she reached her front door.

She walked inside the apartment and spotted Blake sitting on the couch with no shirt on, sparking up a blunt. Immediately, the smell of sex filled her nostrils.

"What was that girl doing up in here? And where is your shirt?" Tiffany said, feeling herself about to cry.

"Fuck is you talking about?" Blake said in a disinterested tone as he rested his legs on the coffee table.

"Who was that girl that just left up out of our house?" Tiffany asked again, with more bass in her voice this time.

"I don't know what you talking about," Blake said with a straight face. "Glad you decided to make it home on time tonight," he said, changing the subject like he always did when he was busted.

"I'm not playing," Tiffany said. She called herself putting her foot down. "Who was she? And what was she doing up in our house?"

"What are you talking about? And what girl?" Blake said again, still with a straight face. When it came to lying, Blake was a professional.

"Fuck that!" Tiffany huffed as she stormed into the bedroom. "I'm tired of this shit!"

Blake quickly hopped up off the couch and followed her into the bedroom.

"Bitch, don't come up in here stomping ya muthafuckin' feet and shit!" he growled as he jacked her up against the wall. "Apologize right now!" he demanded.

"For what? I didn't even do no—"

A sharp punch to the stomach caused Tiffany to double over in pain as Blake jacked her back up against the wall.

"I said apologize. Now!"

"Sorry," she said in a light whisper.

"What you say? I can't hear you," Blake said, taunting her.

"I said sorry," Tiffany said, her voice filled with anger.

Another sharp punch to her stomach caused her to drop to her knees. Again, Blake jacked her back up against the wall.

"I said apologize, bitch!"

"I said sorry." Tiffany sobbed.

"You sorry, what?" Blake growled.

"I'm sorry, Daddy," Tiffany said, the warm tears streaming down her cheeks.

"That's what I thought."

Blake smiled as he punched her in the stomach one last time. He had to make sure she would never run off at the mouth or question him again.

"Get ya ass up," he said, yanking her back up to her feet. "Get in there and make me something to eat."

"Baby, can you please order some food tonight? I'm so tired. I had a long day at work today," she said, a pleading look in her eyes.

"Do it look like I give a fuck if you tired or not?" Blake picked her pocketbook up from the floor. "Get in there and make me something to eat," he said as he took all her money then tossed her pocketbook back down on the floor. "Damn! You made a killing today," he said, stuffing the bills down into his pocket.

Tiffany stood over the stove crying as she prepared a meal for her so-called man. "Fuck this shit!" she said to herself. "This the last time he gon' put his hands on me again."

She didn't know where she was going to go, but she knew she wasn't coming back to this apartment ever again. Tonight was going to be her final night sleeping there.

Quick sat parked a block away from Frank's crib. After tailing the man for the past two days, he was shocked to find out that Frank rolled alone most of the time. He was also shocked when he found out that a man with as much money as Frank lived in a broke down-looking house. Frank was one of them old-school cats who never bought anything big, in fear that a big purchase, or fancy clothes, or a nice ride would lead the police straight to him.

Quick continued to watch the house for a few more hours. After seeing the same pattern for the past two days, he decided that he and Lucky would take the old man out tonight. He made the engine come to life and headed straight for Lucky's crib.

Lucky was sitting on his couch as he watched one of his lady friends get dressed. "Baby, pass me that bottle of Grey Goose from off the counter, please."

The dark-skin girl sucked her teeth as she walked over to the counter. "As much liquor as you drink, I'd think you could fuck me for longer than two minutes."

"What you talking about?" Lucky said, feigning ignorance. The truth was, he had let her give him head so long, as soon as she hopped on top of his dick, he was already about to explode.

"You know I got you the next round."

"I won't hold my breath." Jessica kissed Lucky on the cheek and headed toward the door.

"Where you going?"

"To work. You know some people do have a real job." She winked as she made her exit.

Lucky was sitting on the couch with the TV tuned to *SportsCenter* when he heard a knock at the door. He quickly grabbed the .357 that rested on the couch cushion next to him as he got up and looked through the peephole.

"My nigga, what's popping?" he asked as he gave Quick dap.

"We going to hit Frank tonight," Quick said, stepping inside the crib.

"Tonight?" Lucky repeated. "You sure you wanna do it tonight?"

"Yeah. I been watching how he move for the past two days," Quick told him. "Most of the time, he's alone in his house."

"Fuck it!" Lucky shrugged. "Let's do it."

Quick looked at his watch. It was 7:07 p.m. "I say we get ready and head over there now, watch the crib for about a hour, then make our move."

"Say no more," Lucky said as he disappeared into the back.

He reappeared with two bulletproof vests in his hand. He tossed one to Quick. "You need heat?"

"Nah, I'm straight," Quick said, lifting his shirt and flashing the butt of his 9 mm.

After Lucky strapped on his vest, he then reached under the couch and removed a TEC-9, along with three extra clips. "You ready?"

Quick nodded yes, and the two were out the door.

Lucky parked his hooptie a block away from Frank's house and hit the light. They pulled up right on time to see Frank walking inside his house, talking on his cell phone.

"There go that clown, right there." Lucky pointed. "You wanna hit him now?"

"Nah, let's wait for a minute," Quick suggested as they watched Frank enter the house alone.

Frank stepped inside his crib and gave his main goon, Smokey, dap. "Do me a favor," Frank said as he lit up a cigar. "Get on the phone and get the rest of the crew over here. We need to have a meeting." Frank didn't like how things had been going out in the streets lately, and he thought a meeting was long overdue.

Smokey nodded his head and did as he was told.

"Man!" Lucky huffed. "I'm ready to go in there and handle this nigga," he said, placing his TEC-9 on his lap.

Quick looked down at his watch and saw that almost twenty-five minutes had passed. "Fuck it! Let's do it."

Both men slid out of the vehicle and headed toward the house. On a silent count of three, Quick turned and shot the lock off the front door. Then he moved to the side and watched Lucky kick the front door open.

Lucky barged inside the house and saw Frank sitting on the couch and another man standing in the kitchen by the refrigerator.

Before he got a chance to yell, "Don't move!" he saw the man who stood in the kitchen reach for his waistband. Without hesitation, Lucky squeezed the trigger and felt the gun rattle in his hand, ripping the man they called Smokey to pieces.

Once Smokey's body hit the floor, Lucky turned his TEC-9 on Frank, who was now running toward the back room, but a bullet to the back of his thigh dropped him dead in his tracks. Frank hit the floor, then tried to crawl toward the back room.

"Fuck you think you going?" Lucky flipped the older man over with his foot so he could see his face.

"You young hustlers don't have no respect nowadays," Frank said, wincing in pain.

"Fuck all that! I know you got a stash in here, old man. Where is it?"

Frank spat blood on Lucky's brand-new black Nike boots. "Go suck a AIDS dick!"

"Old man, we can do this the easy way or the hard way."

Frank smiled. "I'm from the old school, so we definitely gonna have to do this the hard way."

Just as the words left Frank's lips, a bullet to the head silenced him once and for all.

Lucky turned around and saw Quick standing there holding a smoking 9 mm.

"Let's go," Quick said. "We didn't come here for all of that."

"Nigga, is you crazy?" Lucky said, looking at Quick like he had two heads. "You know how much money is probably up in here?"

Before Quick could respond, Lucky looked him in his eyes and said, "All I need is two minutes."

Quick looked at Lucky for about four seconds. "Hurry up," he told him as he watched him head toward the back in search of Frank's stash.

Quick paced back and forth, impatiently waiting for Lucky to hurry up and return from the back.

All of a sudden, he heard multiple car doors slamming outside. "What the fuck?" Quick said, a look of confusion on his face as he peeked out the window. "Yo, we got company!" he yelled.

Lucky quickly returned from the back, carrying a garbage bag halfway filled with money. "How many?" he asked, quickly reloading his TEC-9.

"About nine, ten," Quick replied as he aimed his 9 mm toward the door.

"Let's go out the back door," Lucky suggested, and he and Quick dipped out the back door just as Frank's goons were entering the front door.

Once the two made it outside, they sprinted through the grass until they reached the hooptie.

"Here. You drive." Lucky tossed the keys over to Quick as he hopped onto the passenger seat.

Quick got behind the wheel, turned on the car, and gunned the engine. As they drove past the house, Lucky hung out the window and squeezed the trigger on his TEC-9 and shot up the front of the house as the hooptie disappeared into the night.

"That's what the fuck I'm talking about," Lucky said with a smile. He knew the garbage bag between his legs held at least ten grand. Going back for the money was risky, but he felt he did what needed to be done.

Quick parked in front of Lucky's apartment and turned the car off. "We did it," he said, turning to face Lucky.

"This is only the beginning," Lucky said, and the two men got out of the car and went upstairs to count up their earnings.

"Why Me?"

Tiffany kept glancing up at the clock, with only thirty more minutes left until her shift was over. Today wasn't one of her better days. Not only were her feet hurting, but her period also decided to show up today, on top of her not knowing where she was going to rest her head. She might not have known where she was going to stay for the night, but the one thing she did know was she wasn't going to stay with Blake, not one more night.

Tiffany was on her way back to the kitchen when the manager, Mr. Richardson, tapped her on the shoulder. "You free to go home early tonight," he told her, and he disappeared into his office.

Tiffany smiled from ear to ear as she clocked out, grabbed her coat, and headed out the door. At first, she found herself speed-walking, until she remembered that she no longer had to rush anymore.

She went inside the train station to keep warm as she tried to think about where she was going to stay for the night. "Fuck it!" she said to herself as she hopped onto the train. She didn't have any place else to go but to her mother's house. That was the second-to-last place she wanted to go, but what other choices did she have?

When her stop came, Tiffany stepped off the train and power-walked toward her mother's building to get out of the cold. As she walked up to the building, she noticed the regular local drug dealers standing around, looking cool and cold at the same time. They all spoke to her as she entered the building.

As usual, the elevator wasn't working, so Tiffany had to take the steps. She reached her mother's floor, exited the staircase, and headed toward her mother's door. Tiffany took a deep breath as she stood in front of her mother's door for a few seconds before she finally knocked on the door.

Knock! Knock! Knock!

Tiffany heard some feet shuffling on the other side of the door, followed by locks being unlocked. Then the door swung open. Brenda stood in the doorway, looking her one and only daughter up and down. "Fuck you doing here?"

"I need to stay here for a month or two."

"Damn!" Brenda huffed. "I don't get a hello, hi you doing, or nothing?"

"Hello, Mother," Tiffany said dryly.

Just by looking at her mother, Tiffany could tell she was high and drunk. Tiffany and Brenda fought like cats and dogs, the main reason she had moved out at such a young age.

"Now, how long you said you need to stay here for?" Brenda asked, thumping her ashes from her cigarette right onto the floor.

"Just a month or two. Please?"

Brenda examined her daughter's face for a second. "Hmm. I see that man of yours still beating yo' ass." She stepped to the side so Tiffany could enter.

"Thank you," Tiffany said as she entered her mother's house. She knew her mother would never let her hear the end of this, but it was either deal with her mother's bullshit or get her ass beat by Blake. She thought about staying at her mother's house and quickly told herself, "It could always be worse."

"Fuck you standing there like a lost puppy for?" Brenda said loudly. "You know where your room is," she said as she returned to her company, who sat at the kitchen table playing a game of spades while The Temptations hummed through the radio's speakers.

Tiffany walked down the narrow hallway until she reached the room she had called hers once upon a time. Inside the room was a twin-sized mattress that lay on the floor, a dresser, and an old-school nineteen-inch TV that sat on top of the dresser.

Tiffany set her purse down and went back out into the living room. “Excuse me,” Tiffany said.

Brenda and her company, who had cocaine, alcohol, and cigarettes resting openly on the table, looked at her like she had lost her mind.

“Can I help you?” Brenda said, rolling her eyes.

“Where do you keep your sheets so I can make the bed?”

“Sheets?” Brenda echoed, and she laughed way louder than she had to. “I don’t got no sheets. I don’t know if you can tell or not, but I don’t have a lot of overnight company.” Brenda returned her focus to the card game.

Tiffany walked back to her room, cut the TV on, and lay down on the naked mattress that rested on the floor. She looked around the room and silently began to cry. Her life wasn’t supposed to be like this. Some nights, she would just pray to God and ask Him why He had decided to make her life on earth a living hell. “Fuck this!”

she said to herself as she wiped her tears away. "If it ain't a way, then I'm just going to have to make a way," she told herself. The only problem was, she didn't even know where to begin.

Quick looked up and down the block for any signs of police as he made a hand-to-hand sale right out in the street. It had been two weeks since the hit on Frank, and he and Lucky had yet to hear anything from Turf or his peoples.

"I'm telling you," Quick began, "we better hear from this nigga Turf soon, or else."

"Or else what?" Lucky laughed as he watched his breath fog up in the cold. "All we can do is wait. At least we got that money from Frank's crib." Lucky was trying to be cool about the situation, but inside, he felt the same as Quick did. Only, he had a little more patience. "Turf is a man of his word, so he'll show up," he said, speaking in faith.

Quick was about to finish complaining, when he and Lucky saw a black Escalade pull up. Whoever was in the tinted vehicle didn't bother to get out. Instead, they just beeped the horn, signaling for Quick and Lucky to make their way over to the vehicle. Quick and Lucky made their way over to the truck. Before they even reached the truck, the sounds of Young Jeezy could be heard blasting from the Escalade. The driver's window slid down, and Quick saw Wolf sitting behind the wheel and Major Pain sitting over in the passenger seat, bobbing his head to the beat.

"Get in," Wolf said as the tinted window rolled back up.

Quick and Lucky hopped into the backseat, happy to finally be out of the brutal cold weather.

"Damn! Y'all niggas been out there all day?" Major Pain asked with an I-don't-know-how-y'all-do-it look on his face.

"Trap or die," Quick replied, rubbing his hands together. He was excited to finally be about to meet Turf. He had heard plenty of stories about the man, but now he was about to see if he was what everybody said he was.

"Well, today is y'all lucky day," Major Pain told them. He lit up a blunt. "Welcome to the family."

"Welcome to the Family"

Wolf parked the Escalade in front of a church and let the engine die. Quick and Lucky both looked at one another, but neither man said a word. They followed Wolf and Major Pain inside the church and upstairs to the last door on the right.

Wolf knocked on the door, and seconds later, a big, seven-foot, 300–pound, all-muscle monster answered the door.

"Damn, nigga!" Wolf huffed. "Get ya big ugly ass out the doorway," he joked as the foursome entered the nice-sized office.

"Fuck you! You peanut-head muthafucka!" Goliath capped back.

Quick and Lucky stepped inside the office and saw a man that favored the rapper Plies standing over in the corner on the phone. The man they called Turf wore a white long johns shirt with three chains around his neck and a Reds fitted cap on his head.

A Spanish girl sat behind the desk. Only, she wasn't dressed like a secretary, but more like a stripper.

"Yo, I'ma call you back." Turf hung up the phone and turned his attention on Quick and Lucky. "So, these the two that took care of that old head for me?" he asked, already knowing the answer to his question. He walked over and gave both Quick and Lucky dap, looking each man in the eye. "I appreciate what y'all did for me."

"It's nothing," Quick replied.

Turf smiled. "I could use a few good men on the team." He paused to pour himself a drink. "I don't fuck with no bitch-ass, scary niggas, so if y'all ready to get busy, then y'all in the right place."

"We hungry," Lucky said. "So whatever you need us to do, just let us know."

"It's a lot of money out here, gentlemen," Turf said, looking at both men. "Y'all ready to get it?"

"No doubt," Lucky replied with a smile. He knew Turf had found the right men for the job.

Turf was about to take a sip from his glass when he looked up at a smiling Lucky. He asked, "Something funny?"

"I'm just happy to be a part of the team," Lucky explained. "That's all."

"Good," Turf said as he turned toward Goliath. "Pay these brothers so we can get up out of here."

Goliath dug down into his pocket, pulled out a ten thousand–dollar stack, and tossed it to Quick. "Make sure y'all don't spend that all in one spot," he said with a smirk.

"We'll try not to." Quick smiled, happy to finally have a large amount of money in his possession. He quickly divided the stack of money and handed Lucky his half.

"I hope you guys like to party," Turf said.

Once everyone was outside, Turf and Goliath hopped into a Range Rover, while Wolf, Major Pain, Quick, and Lucky hopped back into the Escalade.

Quick sat in the backseat, a relaxed look on his face. He was just thankful that he could make money and not have to stand out on the corner anymore, especially in this type of weather. Whatever needed to be done, he was going to make sure it got done, so that paper could keep coming in. For the rest of the ride, he just stared out the window, thinking about his future and how he was going to handle his money wisely.

Lucky nudged his partner with his elbow. "You a'ight?"

"Yeah, I'm good," Quick answered as the Escalade pulled up into the parking lot right across the street from the club.

Before Wolf and Major Pain hopped out of the Escalade, they made sure they were strapped. "Y'all niggas need heat?" Wolf asked over his shoulder.

"Nah, we got our own shit." Quick patted his waistline. He and Lucky never left home without their straps, just in case anything ever jumped off. They preferred to be safe rather than sorry.

When the crew entered the club, immediately, Quick and Lucky felt like celebrities from all the attention they were getting just because they were with Turf.

"I might can get used to this," Lucky yelled over the loud music with a smile. Even the way the women in the club looked at him was different; he loved the attention.

Quick took a seat in the VIP section and just watched Turf receive all the attention.

"Yo, come here," Turf called Quick over. "You see all this?" he asked, waving at the crowd. "Get used to this. I appreciate what you and ya boy, Lucky, did for me."

"One hand wash the other," Quick replied.

Turf grabbed a bottle of Cîroc Coconut out of the bucket of ice and filled two champagne flutes to the rim. "I got big plans for you and ya man," he said, handing one of the flutes to Quick. "I just need to make sure y'all ready to get y'all hands dirty."

"I don't think you understand." Quick took a sip of his drink. "Me and my man, Lucky, been putting in work for years, and we been doing it for free. Now that we going to be getting paid for it, you don't have nothing to worry about," Quick assured him.

Just as bad as Turf needed Quick and Lucky, they needed the money; so it was an even trade.

"Good." Turf smiled. "Wolf and Major Pain are the two best soldiers I've ever met in my life, but"—he paused so he could take a sip—"we all starting to get a little hot, so some new faces are much needed."

People out in the streets knew not to mess with Turf, and they definitely knew not to mess with his money. Turf had put in way more than enough work, and now it was finally starting to catch up with him. Every cop and detective had him on their list and was gunning for him. They wanted his head on a platter, but Turf was prepared to die before that day ever came.

For the rest of the night, the crew just got their party on like there was no tomorrow. Turf had his twenty-four-hour bodyguard, Goliath, go out into the crowd and pick out twenty of the prettiest women in the club and bring them back to their VIP section.

After about four drinks, Quick was feeling nice. A brown-skin woman with dreads sat next to him, keeping him company. The woman had a pretty face, but Quick was more concerned about the woman's huge ass that looked like it was going to rip through the black spandex she wore.

"Yo, what you said your name was again?" Quick asked with a light slur.

"Ivy." The woman grabbed another bottle of Cîroc Coconut and refilled her and Quick's glasses.

"Damn! You must be trying to take advantage of me tonight," Quick said, openly flirting with the woman. He could tell that Ivy was feeling him, and he, too liked what he was seeing.

From what she had told him, she was a teacher, she had her own crib, she was single, and most importantly, she didn't have a baby daddy or a crazy ex-boyfriend. Seeing as though he didn't have a place to live since Kat had put him out, Ivy looked like she was going to be Quick's next move.

"What's going on over here?" Lucky said, coming toward the couch where Quick and Ivy sat. "And who is this?" He reached for Ivy's hand.

"This is my new friend, Ivy," Quick replied with a smile.

Lucky looked Ivy up and down for a second before he replied. “Good money,” he said as he gave Quick a pound.

As the two stood talking, Major Pain walked over, holding two iced-out chains in his hand. “Y’all are officially a part of the team now,” he said, handing Quick and Lucky both a chain.

Quick smiled as he examined the iced-out cross that rested at the end of the chain before he put it around his neck.

Major Pain gave Quick and Lucky both a pound, followed by a hug.

“So,” Ivy said once Quick sat back down, “what do you guys do for a living?”

“Well, you know,” Quick began, “we got a few businesses popping, and we’ve been expanding a lot lately,” he said, trying to sound like a legit businessman.

Ivy laughed loudly. “You don’t have to lie to me, Quick. I’m not one of these bougie chicks. I’ve heard what Turf does for a living, and I don’t have a problem with that,” she told him. “Shit. These crackers ain’t giving us shit, and a real man ain’t gon’ just sit around broke. So, trust me, I totally understand how you live.”

All Quick could do was smile after that last comment. He loved strong black women, and Ivy appeared to be just that. That alone only made him want her more.

Just as Quick was about to reply to what Ivy had just said, he saw Kat walk up into the VIP section, headed in his direction. He sighed loudly, knowing some dumb shit was soon to follow her arrival.

"Why the fuck you ain't been answering my calls?" Kat said loudly as she stood in front of Quick. Her eyes briefly took in his company then came back to him.

"Fuck is you talking about?" Quick huffed, not wanting to be bothered with this foolishness right now.

"Oh, what, you too busy to answer my calls now?" Kat asked as she turned and looked down at Ivy. "Is this bitch the reason why my calls are being ignored?"

Ivy chuckled at the ignorant woman that stood before her. She took her hand and began rubbing the back of Quick's head as she smiled back at Kat.

Quick knew Kat was about to flip the fuck out, so he hopped up off the couch. "Yo, why you sweating me?" he said in an annoyed tone.

"Why I'm sweating you?" Kat said, her face crumpled up. Her hand quickly shot out and slapped Quick across his face for trying to play her.

"Bitch!" Quick growled as he grabbed Kat by the shirt.

Before shit got out of hand, Goliath came over and escorted Kat out of the VIP area while she cursed at the top of her lungs, struggling to free herself from the big man's grip.

"Sorry about that," Quick apologized to Ivy as Lucky and Wolf broke down laughing. He was embarrassed by the way Kat had showed out.

"It's okay," Ivy said over the rim of her champagne flute. "If those the kind of women you used to dealing with, then you going to love me," she said confidently.

Quick smiled. He could tell just from how Ivy reacted when Kat came over, acting up, that she was a good, mature woman.

"I'm feeling your hair." Quick reached out and touched a few of Ivy's locks.

"Thank you," Ivy replied with a smile.

The DJ then suddenly directed everyone's attention to the front door. "My main man Sosa is in the building!" he announced over the mic.

Everyone's eyes then went toward the entrance. Sosa entered the club, wearing an all-black short-cut mink with the hood over his head, making it hard to see his face, and behind him was his ten-man entourage. Sosa was close friends with one of the rappers from Dipset, so he was looked at as a celebrity, when really, he was nothing but a drug dealer.

The owner of the club placed Sosa and his entourage in the VIP section right next to Turf, the only thing separating the two crews being a red velvet rope. Sosa looked like a younger version of Jay-Z. He got his name from the character Sosa from the movie *Scarface*. He felt nobody was above him in the drug game and decided to run with the name.

Sosa removed his mink and got comfortable as pretty ladies filled the area, followed by bottles of hard liquor. He wore a pair of high-top Uggs with the fur around them, and his jewelry glittered under the light. His main man, Hawk, stood close by, watching his surroundings.

"Yo, ain't that ya man right there?" Hawk asked, motioning his head toward Turf's VIP area.

Sosa looked for a second then smiled as he made his way over there. He unclamped the velvet rope and entered Turf's section.

"My nigga, what's good?" Sosa said as he approached Lucky.

Lucky saw Sosa and went crazy. "Oh shit! My nigga, what's good? Where you been hiding at?"

"I was OT for a little minute. Had to go get this money," Sosa told him. "So, what's good? You trying to get on, or what?"

"Damn!" Lucky said. "I can't even make that move right now. I just started messing with my man Turf."

Sosa looked to see who Lucky was talking about and saw one of his homeboys' little sister, half-naked, sitting up under Turf. "Excuse me for a second," he said, and he walked over to where Turf sat on the couch feeling all over the woman who sat next to him.

As soon as Sosa approached, Goliath, Wolf, and Major Pain rose to their feet, ready for action.

When Hawk saw what was going on, he and the rest of Sosa's goons quickly made their way over to see what was going on.

"Tiffany, get ya shit and get the fuck up outta here," Sosa said to the woman resting on Turf's arm.

Tiffany was getting ready to get up, until Turf pulled her back down.

"Sit down, baby. You don't have to go nowhere," Turf told her.

"Don't make me tell you again," Sosa said, shooting Tiffany a serious look. "If your brother wasn't locked up right now, you know you wouldn't dare let him catch you dead in a place like this."

"Fuck is you? Her bodyguard?" Turf huffed. "You acting like I'm forcing her to be here."

"I wasn't talking to you," Sosa said coldly. He knew exactly who Turf was, but he couldn't care less about him or his crew. Sosa wasn't about to let his man Bullet's little sister be out here acting like a ho, at least not while he was around.

Turf quickly stood to his feet. "Fuck you talking to like that?" he asked, he and Sosa standing nose-to-nose, both crews on edge and ready to pop off at any second.

Tiffany quickly jumped up between the two. "I'm leaving," she said, looking at Sosa. She didn't want to see any bloodshed because of her.

"You don't gotta go nowhere, baby," Turf told her.

"I'll catch up with you another time." Tiffany squeezed through the crowd and headed toward the exit.

Turf shook his head. "Damn! All this over a bitch?" he said, trying to get under Sosa's skin.

Sosa sighed loudly as he shook his head and walked back over to his section.

"That's what the fuck I thought!" Turf poured himself another drink and went back to partying.

Sosa poured himself a drink. He was pissed at how Turf had just tried to disrespect him. If you were on Sosa's team, then you were family. So he was taking it as Turf trying to disrespect one of his family members.

"How you wanna handle this?" Hawk asked as he sat down next to Sosa. He had known Sosa for a long time, so he already knew what his look meant.

Sosa finished his drink before responding. "When they come outside, we going to air this whole shit out." He grabbed a bottle of Rosé from the bucket of ice and walked over to Lucky. "Yo, I'm out," he said, giving Lucky dap. "I'ma get up you with later," Sosa said, as he and his crew made their exit.

Once Sosa and his crew left, Turf called Lucky over. "You know that muthafucka?"

"I went to high school with him back in the day," Lucky said, trying to downplay it. He liked Sosa and didn't want to see the two go head to head.

"Good. 'Cause he was about to get his fuckin' head pounded in," Turf said, meaning every word.

Turf had noticed that the crowd began to get smaller and smaller. "This bitch starting to die down," he said.

"You wanna get something to eat when we get up outta here?" Quick asked.

"Um, I do have to go to work in the morning." Ivy smiled. "But I am kind of hungry," she said, not wanting the night to end.

Lucky walked up. "Yo, we up outta here."

Turf and the whole crew got up and headed toward the exit. They had a few girls with them and planned on having an after-party back at a hotel room. This was what they did on a nightly basis.

Turf stepped outside, and the cold slapped him in the face, disrespecting the thin sweater he wore. As soon as they hit the curb, gunshots erupted, and everyone got low to the ground, not wanting to get shot.

Quick grabbed Ivy and pulled her down to the ground. He covered her with his body as he pulled his 9 mm from his waistband and returned fire.

Turf hid behind a parked car as he pulled his .40-cal from his waistband, and Major Pain and Wolf returned fire, making it sound like World War III.

Sosa hung out the passenger window of his truck with his finger pressed down on his TEC-9, hitting anything moving, while Hawk and the rest of his goons did the same thing. Sosa shot women and bouncers, along with a few men from Turf's crew as his truck burned rubber down the street.

Major Pain and Wolf chased after the truck, letting off shots until the truck was no longer in sight. Once the gunfire ceased, Turf and Goliath hopped into the Range Rover and peeled off.

"Come on, we gotta go!" Ivy yelled as she grabbed Quick's hand and led him toward her Dodge Charger that sat parked on the corner.

Quick looked over his shoulder and saw Lucky hop into the Escalade with Wolf and Major Pain. Once he knew Lucky was safe, he hopped onto the passenger seat of the Charger. Ivy turned on the car and immediately gunned the engine, leaving the crime scene.

"You a'ight?" Quick asked, looking over at Ivy's body, to see if she was bleeding.

Ivy kept looking through her rearview mirror as she drove, making sure no police were following her. "Yeah, I'm fine."

"Damn! Slow this muthafucka down," Quick said, afraid that Ivy would attract police to them with her reckless driving.

"Sorry." Ivy let up on the gas pedal a bit.

Fifteen minutes later, Ivy pulled into her parking spot in front of her apartment. "Well, this is it," she said, and she and Quick hopped out of the car and headed toward the front door.

As soon as the two stepped inside the apartment, they were all over one another. Quick and

Ivy kissed as they ripped one another's clothes off, exploring each other's bodies.

Quick lifted Ivy up, and she quickly wrapped her legs around his waist as they continued to kiss. He carried her into the bedroom and laid her down on the bed, where he fondled her soft breasts.

Ivy kicked off her expensive three-inch heels as she felt Quick snatch off her bra and stuffed one of her pierced nipples inside his mouth. She moaned as she felt her juice box began to get extra wet.

After sucking on both her titties, Quick smoothly pulled Ivy's spandex off, revealing her sexy, meaty thighs and calves. He spread her legs wide open and began kissing and licking on her inner thighs, but she got tired of the anticipation and guided his head in the right direction.

Quick licked and sucked all over Ivy's clitoris as he listened to her moan in pleasure. He slipped his finger inside her warm, soaking wet pussy, while he continued to suck and lick all over her clit, forcing her to come for him.

Once Quick had made Ivy come, that made her want the dick even more. Quick rolled on a condom and watched Ivy climb on top of him, straddling him backward, cowgirl style.

"Damn!" Quick moaned as he entered Ivy's walls.

Ivy violently bounced up and down, loving how Quick filled her up and how he felt inside of her. And he watched as Ivy's ass bounced up and down against his torso.

Quick smacked her ass as he began talking shit. "That's right. Ride this dick," he said, smacking her ass again. "I want you to come all over this dick."

Ivy's moans became louder and louder. The more she moaned, the harder and faster she bounced.

"Oooh shit!" Quick groaned as he exploded. "Damn!" he said, breathing heavily.

Ivy crawled up toward Quick and kissed him on the lips. "Thank you," she said, and she got up and hopped into the shower.

Quick got up from the bed and followed Ivy inside the bathroom and joined her in the shower. There, they took turns washing each other up before they got out and hopped into the bed. Minutes later, both of them were knocked out.

“Here We Go Again”

Tiffany hopped out of the shower feeling good. The way she was living was disgusting and horrible, but she simply told herself, “It could always be worse.” She looked in the mirror and smiled. She was starting to like what she was seeing. She no longer had bruises or black eyes, and she was finally able to see her true beauty.

Another reason she was feeling good was because she finally had some money. Since she had been away from Blake, she had managed to save up $1,600, the most money she had seen at one time, except for when she got her income tax check.

Tiffany danced around her room as she got ready for work. Everything was good, until she heard a knock at her room door. Instantly, she knew it could only one person.

“Come in,” she yelled.

Brenda entered her daughter’s room with an unlit cigarette dangling from her mouth. “Let your mother borrow forty dollars," she said with her hand out. "I know you got it."

"You don't know what I got," Tiffany capped back, not liking the way her mother came at her.

"I know you got something," Brenda said, looking Tiffany up and down. "You go out this house every muthafuckin' day. Shit, you better have something."

Tiffany didn't feel like arguing, so she gave Brenda the forty dollars just to get her up out of her face.

All I need is two more weeks, and I'm up outta here, she thought to herself as she finished getting dressed. Then she headed out the door before Brenda could ask her for anything else.

Tiffany made it to work with a smile on her face. She couldn't remember the last time she had been this happy. Ever since Blake had been out of her life, she was stress and worry free.

As she walked over toward her sections, she spotted the handsome man she had seen a few weeks back. "How you gentlemen doing today?" she asked with a bright smile. "Can I get y'all something to drink to start off with?"

Quick smiled. The last time he and Lucky were there, he didn't remember the waitress looking him dead in his eyes when she spoke. He was actually waiting for her eyes to drop down to the floor, but when they didn't, he was kind of taken by surprise.

"Yeah, I'll take a orange juice, thanks," he said as the two kept eye contact for a few seconds longer.

Tiffany turned and faced Lucky. "And you?"

"I'll take a orange juice too," Lucky replied.

Once Tiffany walked away, Lucky got down to business. "Turf called and said he got our first job for us."

"Word?"

"Yeah," Lucky replied. "This is our chance to earn our keep around here, so whatever we have to do, we gonna have to go overboard."

"Don't we always?"

Quick smiled as Tiffany returned with their drinks. He and Lucky quickly placed their orders then got back down to business.

"You think we going to have to clap something?" Quick asked.

Lucky shrugged nonchalantly. "Probably." The truth was, he didn't care what they had to do. As long as they were getting paid, Lucky was down.

***

Blake pulled up to Tiffany's job and hopped out of his car with a serious attitude. He slammed his car door and walked inside the restaurant. He skipped right past the hostess and immediately spotted Tiffany carrying two plates in her hand. He walked right to her and smacked both of the plates out of her hand then wrapped his hands around her throat as he hemmed her up against the wall, trying to choke the life out of her right there in the restaurant.

"Bitch, you thought you could get away from me?" Blake growled as he squeezed even tighter. "You belong to me!" he growled through clenched teeth. "As soon as you get off, you better bring your muthafuckin' ass straight home!" And he tossed Tiffany down to the floor.

"Hey, is everything all right over here?" a white waiter asked as he looked at Tiffany lying down on the floor.

Blake quickly stole on the white boy, dropping him with one punch. "Fuck you mean, is everything all right?" he yelled, looking down at the unconscious man. He then turned and snatched Tiffany back up to her feet by her shirt. "Don't make me have to come up here again," he warned.

Just as Blake was about to smack the shit out of her, Quick caught his hand before he could even bring it down. "Fuck is you doing?" he said, pushing him away from Tiffany.

"Nigga, don't put your fuckin' hands on me. Is you crazy?" Blake puffed up. He knew his chances of winning a fistfight with Quick weren't good, and he also knew that Quick was more than likely strapped, but he had to save face.

"You wanna get busy?" Quick removed his 9 mm from his waistline right there in the restaurant, all the while glaring at Blake.

Before Blake could say another word, Quick smacked the shit out of him in front of everybody.

Blake touched his lip, and his hand came away bloody. He smiled as he nodded his head up and down. "I'ma see you again," he said as he backed out of the restaurant, never taking his eyes off Quick.

"I ain't hard to find," Quick said confidently, sticking his racht back down into his waistband. He then turned his attention on Tiffany. "You a'ight?"

"Yes," Tiffany said as the tears flowed down her face. She knew if she didn't go back home to Blake, he would definitely be back at her job again the following day. Then she wouldn't even have a job. But now, if she did go back to him, he was sure to whip her ass, especially since Quick had embarrassed him in front of her.

"Was that your boyfriend?" Quick asked when he noticed Tiffany wouldn't stop crying. Right then and there, he knew that something serious was going on in her life.

Before Quick could say another word, Mr. Richardson came from the back. "What the hell is going on out here?"

Once Quick saw the police pull up to the restaurant, he and Lucky quickly made their exit.

"You a crazy muthafucka." Lucky laughed. "Trust me, don't no nigga come up to a bitch job and beat her ass for no reason," he said, and the two slid into the hooptie and pulled off.

"Nah, she don't strike me as the type," Quick said, staring out the window.

Lucky huffed. "Shit, you probably hurt her more than you helped her, 'cause you know he gon' fuck her up when she get home."

Quick didn't reply. He just stared out the window and enjoyed the ride as Plies pumped through the speakers. Inside, he felt bad for Tiffany and was only trying to help her, but he knew what Lucky said was true. He had probably made her situation even worse than it already was.

Lucky parked his car behind the church, and he and Quick hopped out and entered the church.

"What's good?" Lucky said as he and Quick gave each member in the office dap.

Lucky and Quick took seats at the round table as they waited for Turf to speak.

"That nigga Sosa," Turf began. "How well do you know him?" He looked at Lucky.

"That was my first time seeing him in a mad long time," Lucky replied. "We just used to go to school together."

"I got something for that clown." Turf smiled. "But I have a job for you two."

"Wassup?" Quick asked, sitting up in his chair. Whatever Turf needed them to do, he was ready to do it and get it over with.

Turf leaned back in his chair. "We have a snitch on the team. I just got word that that nigga Roach has been running his mouth."

"What's the nigga résumé?" Lucky asked.

Goliath walked over and handed Lucky a piece of paper with all of Roach's info on it.

"The one thing I can't stand is a snitch," Turf said, sternly looking at everyone who sat at the round table. His eyes then went back to Quick and Lucky. "I need y'all to take care of this for me. Oh, and he owe me some money too," Turf suddenly reminded himself. "Bring that back to me as well."

Turf tossed Quick a stack of money. "That's ten thousand for y'all to split. The more work you two put in, the more you'll get paid. You just gotta work your way up from the bottom first."

"No problem," Quick said, and he and Lucky got up and made their exit.

Quick handed Lucky his share of the money as they slid into the hooptie.

"Shit. This five thousand apiece shit is whack," Lucky complained as he pulled away from the church.

"Five thousand a day seems good to me," Quick said, counting out his money. He had been saving all of his money, so it didn't matter to him. Besides, five thousand a day was more than he was making before Turf had put him on the team.

"You thinking too small," Lucky said as he maneuvered through the New York City traffic. "I definitely ain't trying to be a worker for the rest of my life." He figured, if he was going to be in it, he might as well be in it all the way. Working for Turf for a long period of time definitely wasn't in his plans.

Lucky pulled up in front of Roach's house and killed the engine. He hopped out and walked over to the trunk, from where he removed his TEC-9 and stuck it down into his pants as he and Quick walked up to the front door.

Quick rang the doorbell and patiently waited for someone to answer the door.

Seconds later, Roach answered the door. "Yes, can I help y'all?" he asked, looking the two up and down.

"Yeah. We here to pick up the money you have for Turf," Quick said politely.

"Yeah, yeah, yeah. Come on in," Roach said, stepping to the side so the men could enter. "So, you the two new guys, huh? I've been waiting to meet y'all. I'm Roach," he said, introducing himself.

"We would love to chitchat with you, but we gotta get out of here," Quick said, as he and Lucky stood in the kitchen.

"Okay, no problem. Give me one second, and I'll be right back," Roach said, and he disappeared up the steps.

Quick and Lucky waited patiently for him to return.

Ten minutes later, Roach returned downstairs with a smile on his face. "Sorry about the wait, but I had to count up that money," he said, holding out the book bag.

Quick gladly accepted the book bag. "Can I have a glass of water before I go, please?"

"Sure," Roach said, and he turned to head toward the refrigerator.

As soon as he turned around, Quick pulled out his 9 mm and shot him in the back of the head, and Roach's body dropped face-first to the floor as blood stained the refrigerator door.

Just as Quick and Lucky headed for the door, they heard footsteps coming down the stairway. Lucky quickly pulled out his TEC-9 and aimed it at the bottom of the steps.

Roach's wife and two little daughters came downstairs and froze when they saw two men standing in their kitchen with guns. Roach's wife looked down and saw her husband laid out on the floor and began to cry.

Quick looked at the woman and two kids and stuck his gun back into his waistband. "Come on, let's get outta here," he said.

"A'ight," Lucky replied, and he squeezed the trigger, waving his arms back and forth.

Quick watched in horror as the TEC-9 bullets chopped up Roach's wife and two daughters, leaving their bodies smoking.

When the two got back inside the car, Quick just glared at Lucky.

"What?" Lucky said as he pulled off. "They saw our face."

Quick didn't reply. He just kept quiet, not believing what Lucky had just done.

"I just saved our asses," Lucky said. He didn't want to kill Roach's wife and kids, but he felt he was left with no choice. They saw his and Quick's faces, so they had to go.

Lucky pulled up in front of Ivy's apartment and placed the car in park. "You chilling in the crib for the rest of the night?"

"Yeah, I'm done for the night." Quick gave Lucky dap and headed inside the crib.

"Same Ole, Same Ole"

Tiffany stepped off the bus, and instantly, her stomach began to hurt just from all the pain and drama that she knew wasn't far away. She took her time as she walked into the projects. After what had gone down earlier at the restaurant, she knew Blake was not going to be in a good mood at all. She didn't want to go back to him, but she felt as if she didn't have a choice. No matter where she went, she knew Blake would find her.

She stepped off the elevator and nervously walked down the hallway until she reached the door. She stuck her key inside the lock, unlocked the door, and entered the apartment. As soon as she stepped foot into the apartment, she spotted Blake sitting on the couch with a blunt in his mouth and a bottle of Absolut on the coffee table in front of him.

Blake stood up off the couch, but Tiffany spoke before he got a chance to say a word.

"Baby, I'm sorry about what happened earlier. I swear, I didn't mean for that to happen," she pleaded. She was just hoping that he believed her.

"So you left me to go fuck with that nigga Quick?" Blake asked in a calm tone as he slowly walked over to Tiffany. He could tell she was terrified, just from the look on her face.

"No, baby. I was at my mother's house, I swear."

The look on Blake's face told Tiffany that he didn't believe a word she said.

Blake's arm shot out, and Tiffany flinched, thinking he was about to hit her, but instead, he snatched her pocketbook. He removed the rest of the sixteen hundred dollars she had saved up and tossed her pocketbook down to the floor.

"You walking around with all this cash, while I'm sitting at home broke? That's how you gon' do me after all I've done for you?"

"Nigga, you ain't never did shit for me," Tiffany wanted to say, but instead, she said, "I didn't know you was broke. I thought you was doing good selling the weed you had bought."

"I was so stressed out about you leaving me, so I had to smoke all of it." Blake counted out all of Tiffany's hard-earned money, then stuffed it down into his pocket. "Now back to this nigga

Quick," he said, looking Tiffany in the eyes. "How long you been with this nigga?"

"I swear, baby, I haven't—"

Smack! A slap to Tiffany's face stunned her.

"Bitch, don't you even think about lying to me," Blake said. "Now I'm only going to ask you one more time: How long have you been dealing with that nigga Quick?"

"I'm telling you the truth. I don't even know him. I saw him at the restaurant a few—"

Smack! Another slap to Tiffany's face caused her to stumble back against the wall.

Tiffany saw that Blake was about to strike her again, so she said, "Okay, okay, okay. I've been talking to him since I left." She lied for fear of getting hit again. She knew if she told Blake what he wanted to hear, he would stop hitting her. Blake liked to feel like he was always right about everything, so she played along, hoping he wouldn't hit her anymore.

"I'm sorry. I swear, baby, from now on, it's only going to be me and you, just like old times," Tiffany said, forcing a smile to try and ease some of the tension.

"Just like old times, right?"

Blake turned and smacked her in her face repeatedly. His smacks turned into punches as Tiffany curled up on the floor crying, and begging him to stop. The more she begged, the more he beat her. He appeared to get more pleasure because she was begging.

Blake ripped off all of Tiffany's clothes and looked down at her like she was nothing. "Get over here and suck on your dick!" He watched her crawl to him on her knees.

"I don't know how many times I gotta tell you"—Blake paused as he whipped out his dick—"you belong to me!" he growled as he stood in front of Tiffany and watched her perform her oral duties.

The whole time, Blake degraded her while she slobbed and sucked all over his dick. As soon as he felt himself about to come, he quickly pulled out and came all over her face.

"You belong to me!" Blake huffed as he jerked on his dick, trying to get every last drop on Tiffany's face. His plan was to make Tiffany feel like she was worthless and wasn't shit, and so far, it was working. "You belong to me, bitch! Let me hear you say it," Blake said, looking down at Tiffany, who was still on her knees, semen covering her face.

"I belong to you," Tiffany said in a defeated tone.

"You belong to me, what?"

"I belong to you, Daddy."

A smirk danced on Blake's lips as he walked past Tiffany, leaving her on her knees, and went to the bedroom.

Once the coast was clear, Tiffany stood to her feet and made her way to the bathroom, where the first thing she did was wash her face. She then turned the shower water on as she just sat on the toilet and cried her eyes out. She didn't know what she was going to do, but there was only one way she saw herself leaving Blake. She didn't want to do it, but she didn't really feel like she had a choice. She was going to have to kill him.

Quick woke up with a smile on his face. He could smell breakfast in the air. He slid out of the bed and made his way to the kitchen, where he saw Ivy standing in front of the stove wearing nothing but a thong. He smiled as he went into the bathroom to wash his face and brush his teeth.

Quick stepped out of the bathroom and entered the living room, where Ivy had both of their plates prepared at the kitchen table.

"About time you woke up." Ivy smiled and kissed Quick on the lips.

Quick sat down at the table. In front of him were turkey bacon, pancakes, and scrambled eggs.

"I got me enough money to get me a place of my own now," Quick said after he dug into his food. He liked living with Ivy. She was a good woman and fun to be around, but he just felt like he was invading her space.

"Why you looking for a new place?" Ivy asked, shocked. "What? You don't like staying here with me?"

"Of course, I do. I just thought you would like your space back."

"That doesn't make any sense," Ivy said, not understanding. She loved living with Quick and thought he was perfect for her. Now, out of the blue, she couldn't understand why he just wanted to leave. "Is it that you don't want to be with me anymore?"

"Yes, I still want to be with you," Quick replied. "Honestly, I just need a crib to stash my money in, and I'm definitely not keeping it in here."

"What's wrong with the bank?" Ivy dug into her food.

Quick looked at her like she was insane. "I'll never put my money in a bank." Quick needed to be in control of his money, since the thought of someone else handling his money for him didn't sit well with him. "Nah," he said. "I need a crib."

"So what's all this shit about me needing my space?" Ivy asked with a slight attitude.

"I'm just saying . . . I know you was used to having your own crib, and I just moved in unexpected—"

"Baby, I don't want you to go," Ivy said, quickly cutting him off. She whined like a baby as she pushed away from the table, walked over, and squatted down between Quick's legs.

"Is there anything I can do to make you stay?" she asked in a sexually charged voice. She pulled out Quick's dick and worked him into stiffness with her hands.

Quick smiled. "I ain't going nowhere," he said as he watched Ivy take him inside of her mouth slowly.

Ivy sucked, licked, and slobbed all over Quick's dick, jerking it the whole time. She began to jerk faster as her hands sped up. She moaned loudly as she looked up at Quick the whole time, until he filled her mouth with his fluids.

Ivy walked over to the garbage can and spat before she spoke. "Yo' ass ain't going nowhere," she said with a smile.

Quick smiled as he answered his ringing cell phone. "Yo."

"I need to see you and your partner at the spot in a hour," Turf said, and he ended the call.

Quick hung up the phone and texted Lucky to let him know that Turf needed to see the two of them.

"You got something you need to do today?" Quick stripped out of his clothes and turned the shower water on.

"Nope," Ivy sang as she flopped down on the bed. She loved looking at Quick's naked body.

Quick hopped into the bathroom, took a quick shower, and then got dressed. He peeled off a few hundred-dollar bills and tossed them on the bed. "I need you to go find me an apartment today," he told Ivy.

"I got you, baby," she said, and she took the money and placed it on top of the dresser. "One or two bedrooms?"

"One should do," Quick said. Then he kissed Ivy on the lips and headed out the door.

An hour later, Quick pulled up and parked his hooptie in the back of the church. When he stepped out of the car, he saw Goliath by the back door, waiting for him.

"What's good?" Quick asked, giving the big man dap.

Once Goliath saw that Quick was alone, he asked him, "Where ya man Lucky at?"

"I don't know." Quick shrugged. "I texted him and told him Turf wanted to meet us."

When the two made it to the office, everyone was there except for Lucky. Quick took his seat and waited for Turf to begin the meeting.

"Where's Lucky?" Turf asked with a stone-faced look.

"I don't know," Quick replied. "I texted him and told him that you wanted to meet us at the spot in a hour."

From the look on Turf's face, Quick could tell that something was wrong.

"I had a few of my men follow you and Lucky to see if I could trust you two," Turf said. Then he added, "It turns out, Lucky ain't who he says he is."

"Not who he says he is?" Quick echoed. He knew for a fact that Lucky wasn't a cop, nor was he a snitch. After all, he had seen him lay his murder game down without even thinking twice, so he really didn't understand what Turf was trying to say.

"I had one of my men follow you and follow him," Turf said. "Come to find out, your friend Lucky been hanging out with Sosa. Long story short, Lucky has to go." Turf tried to read Quick's facial expression. "Do you have a problem with that?"

"Yeah," Quick replied. "I grew up with him. I can't just kill somebody I've known all my life."

"We going to hit up Sosa's house tonight. If Lucky's there, then oh well." Turf shrugged. He didn't have time to play games. "Either you in or you out," he said, all eyes on Quick.

Quick knew if he said he didn't want anything to do with it, Turf and his crew would probably kill him right where he stood. "Fuck it!" he said. "Count me in."

Turf smiled. "I know you are new to this business. But sometimes it doesn't matter who it is. If they not moving how they supposed to, then they have to go. This is a business—a million-dollar-a-year business—and if you want to make it in this business, sometimes you might have to do something you don't want to. But you have to do it for the business."

Quick nodded his head, indicating that he understood. He understood what Turf was saying, but Lucky was like a brother to him, and if Lucky was on the wrong end of his gun, he wouldn't be able to pull the trigger.

Turf suddenly remembered to tell Quick, "Oh yeah, you getting a promotion today. I'ma need you to run the trap house that Roach used to run. Can you handle that?"

Quick nodded his head yes, and Goliath handed him the address to the trap house.

"Go handle that, and we'll call you later when it's time to handle that nigga Sosa," Goliath said.

Quick exited the church, hopped into his whip, and peeled off. He couldn't believe what he had just heard. Why didn't Lucky let him know what he was doing? And why would he be dealing with Sosa, especially after the shootout that had gone down a few weeks ago?

Quick pulled out his cell phone and dialed Lucky's number, but it went straight to voice mail. He wanted to give Lucky a heads-up. Quick pulled up a block away from the trap house and let the engine die. He loaded his 9 mm, stuck it down into his waistband, walked around to the back door, and knocked lightly.

A scrawny-looking teenager named Spike answered the door. He barked, "How many times I gotta tell y'all muthafuckas not to knock on the back door?"

Quick looked over both shoulders then stole on Spike, pushing his way inside the trap house. He pulled out his 9 mm and put it to the teenager's head.

"Take all the money," Spike said, sounding like a bitch. "It's in the back room."

"Shut ya punk ass up." Quick stuck his 9 mm back down into his waistband. "I'm the new nigga in charge. Turf put me in charge of running this place."

"Oh," Spike said. "Good. 'Cause I was just about to whip ya ass."

Quick shook his head as he looked around the place. He saw fiends scattered all around the living room, getting high. He checked the back rooms and found baggies and heaps of trash lying around on the floor. On the dresser was a duffel bag filled with crumpled bills, mostly tens and fives and a few twenties here and there.

"How much money in that bag?" Quick asked.

Spike shrugged. "I don't know. Why?"

"From now on, I don't want no more than ten thousand in this house at a time," Quick said.

Just then, Quick heard someone knocking at the door. He walked through the pack of fiends and answered the door.

A filthy, ashy-looking man stepped inside. "Hey, my main man," he said, trying to give Quick dap.

Quick closed the door and looked at the fiend until he put his hand down.

"Hey, where's Roach at?" the fiend asked.

"We under new management now," Quick told the dirty fiend. "And from now on, don't knock on the front door. Start using the back door. Spike, come serve this nigga and get him the fuck outta here. Matter of fact, I want all these fiends up outta here. This is a trap house, not a muthafuckin' crackhouse!"

"Damn! That's fucked up," Willie grumbled as he paid for his crack and left.

"Get these ugly muthafuckas up outta here while I count this money," Quick huffed.

Quick began separating the crumpled bills. He put the fives, tens, and twenties in separate piles. After counting the money, the first thing he planned on doing was washing his hands. He had never seen such dirty money before in his life.

"Dirty money is better than no money," Quick told himself as he zipped up the duffel bag.

Quick returned to the living room, where he saw Spike sitting down, skimming through a magazine. "So, this all you do all day?" Quick asked, helping himself to a seat.

"Pretty much." Spike shrugged. "All I do is wait for the money to come. The shit is like clockwork. Every two minutes, it's a knock at the door."

"I'ma get us some lookouts and post them on each corner to let us know when cops are coming and look out for stickup kids," Quick said, thinking out loud.

"Stickup kids?" Spike chuckled. "Ain't nobody stupid enough to try and rob one of Turf spots."

"Trust me," Quick said, turning to face Spike. "Wherever there's money, the stickup kids aren't too far behind."

Quick heard another knock at the door. He watched as Spike just opened the door without looking through the peephole. He made a mental note to put up a few cameras, so he could see who was coming and going out of his spot at all times, since he didn't like surprises.

After Spike finished serving the fiend, he saw Quick staring at him. "What?"

"You strapped?" Quick asked.

Spike shook his head no.

"You up in here like a sitting duck." Quick laughed. "Listen, I'm up outta here. I'll be back tomorrow," he said, shaking his head as he made his way back out the back door.

"Old-school niggas swear they know it all," Spike said to himself once Quick was gone.

Willie left the trap house and looked over both shoulders as he hopped into a black van parked at the end of the block.

"What's the word?" Detective Davis asked.

"Man," Willie began, "they got this new cat up in there. He done changed everything all around inside there."

"New cat?" Detective Davis said, sitting up. "What happened to Roach?"

"I don't know." Willie shrugged. "All I know is, I don't like this new cat. Matter of fact, there he go right there." He pointed out Quick to Detective Davis.

Detective Davis watched as Quick walked over to his car, hopped in, and drove off. "So that's the new guy, huh," he said to himself. "Don't worry. I'ma find out exactly who he is," he said as he watched Quick drive right past the van.

Detective Davis reached down into his pocket and pulled out a twenty-dollar bill. "Here," he said, handing Willie the bill. "Keep up the good work. Keep your eyes on that new guy for me." Detective Davis watched Willie hop out of the van and take off down the street.

Detective Davis pulled off and headed home. For the entire ride, his mind was on the new guy. He didn't know what it was about the new guy, but it just seemed like he was going to be a problem.

Detective Davis stepped out of the van and stepped inside his one-bedroom apartment. Inside his living room, he had no furniture, just pictures of Turf and every member of his crew posted up on his wall. So far, he didn't have a case, but he was determined to build one. Detective Davis was good at what he did. He was the kind of cop who lived and breathed his job. If he wasn't on a big case, he wouldn't know what to do with his life.

Detective Davis, who kind of favored the actor Mel Gibson in his younger days, walked over to his refrigerator and took out a two-day-old slice of pizza and a Budweiser, and he sat down on the floor and ate, staring at the pictures that hung on his wall.

When Quick left the trap house, he didn't really feel like going home just yet, so he made a detour and decided he would go get him something to eat. He pulled into the IHOP parking lot and shut off the engine.

As soon as he stepped into the restaurant, he spotted Tiffany carrying a plate in each hand. The hostess escorted him to his seat and then he skimmed over the menu.

When he saw Tiffany approaching, he looked up from the menu. "Hey. What's up?" he said, not really knowing what to say.

"Hey," Tiffany said, and her eyes dropped down to the floor. She was still embarrassed about what had happened the last time Quick was there and was surprised he even still spoke to her.

"How you been?" Quick asked, noticing the red marks on Tiffany's neck. She looked like someone had been strangling her.

"I been cool," she replied with a weak smile. "You ready to order?"

"Yeah, I'll take my usual . . . steak and fries." Quick held out the menu, so she could take it.

"Would you like something to drink with that?" Tiffany asked, taking back the menu.

"I want to take you out on a date," Quick said, ignoring her question.

"I don't think that will be a good idea." Tiffany walked off toward the kitchen.

Quick watched as Tiffany disappeared through the double doors to the kitchen. He couldn't understand why women would rather stay in an abusive relationship, when they had a chance to get out.

Tiffany walked back into the kitchen, grabbed a sharp knife, and stuck it down into her apron. The next time Blake tried to put his hands on her, she was going to kill him. Her mind was already made up.

Tiffany liked Quick, who seemed like a nice guy, but right now, she had too much going on in her life to be thinking about going out on a date, the last thing on her mind. She was about to take someone's life if she had to, and everything else just had to wait.

As Quick sat waiting for his food, he received a text message from Major Pain, telling him it was time to meet up. He stuck his phone back down into his pocket just as he saw Tiffany walking toward his table, carrying his plate.

"I'm sorry. I'ma need this to go," he said politely.

Tiffany walked toward the back and returned with a take-home box and a bag.

"Thank you," Quick said, and he dropped three twenty-dollar bills down on the table and left in a hurry.

Tiffany watched Quick until he pulled out of the parking lot. She was thankful that he had saved her from Blake the last time he was there, but she didn't think that a date right now would be a good idea.

She walked to the back to Mr. Richardson's office. "Hey. You got a minute?" she asked.

"What's on your mind?" Mr. Richardson set down the paperwork he was going over and gave Tiffany his undivided attention.

"I'm not feeling too good. Is it all right if I take the rest of the night off?" she asked, putting on her best I-don't-feel-good face.

"Sure," Mr. Richardson said. "But I'll need you here on time tomorrow."

"You got it." Tiffany smiled as she walked around the desk to give her boss a thank-you hug.

Then she went and grabbed her things and headed home. All she wanted to do was go home and relax. She was praying that Blake didn't start no shit tonight because, the way she was feeling right now, she could kill him twice.

Tiffany hopped off the bus and headed down the block. For some reason, tonight she was feeling good. In her pocket, she held the knife that she had stolen from work extra tight as she entered her building. Tiffany had no idea what would pop off tonight, and to be honest, she really didn't care. She was sick and tired of being sick and tired. At some point in one's life, a person has to put their foot down and say enough is enough, and tonight was that night for her.

She stepped off the elevator and slowly walked down the narrow hallway until she reached her door, taking a deep breath as she stuck her key through the lock and entered the place she called home.

Tiffany stepped inside and smiled when she saw that Blake wasn't home. She thanked God over and over again, because she really didn't feel like being bothered with Blake's bullshit tonight, and honestly, she didn't want to have to kill him, but she would if she had to.

She walked into her room and stuck the knife down into the back of her drawer, underneath some clothes. She knew she probably wouldn't see Blake for a few days, until he spent all of the sixteen hundred dollars.

She stripped down out of her clothes, walked to the bathroom, and ran her some bathwater. She just planned on relaxing tonight. She stepped into the tub and got comfortable as the hot water made her feel better.

She rested her head on the back of the tub. She remembered when she and Blake had gotten together. He used to be such a nice guy. It seemed like he just started changing overnight. He was insecure and didn't know how to handle being with an attractive woman. If she spoke to anybody, she had to explain herself, like she was a child. His child. No matter what she told him, he never believed her, and he would question her about her every move. Then came the physical abuse.

Tiffany's thoughts were interrupted when she heard the front door open then close. Then she heard footsteps, and seconds later, Blake poked his head through the bathroom door.

"Hey, baby," he said as he came into the bathroom. He leaned down and kissed her on the cheek. "What you doing home so early?"

"I wasn't feeling too good, so I left work early," she told him as she stood and grabbed her towel so she could dry off.

Tiffany was surprised that Blake was in such a good mood. Usually, he'd come home drunk and in a grumpy mood.

"I'll be back later," Blake said, heading for the door.

Tiffany didn't ask where he was going, because she couldn't care less. *As long as he didn't start no shit, it wouldn't be no shit,* she thought as she went and climbed into the bed, where she relaxed for the rest of the night.

"Party Time"

Quick pulled up to the address where Major Pain had told him to meet him. When he pulled up, he saw three vans parked out front and around twelve to fifteen rough-looking men standing around, dressed in all black. He hopped out of his car and walked up. From what he saw, each man held an automatic weapon.

"Glad you could finally make it," Wolf said with a smirk on his face. In his hand he held a MAC-11.

Quick gave Wolf dap then moved on to Major Pain. "What's the word?" he asked.

"This fucka Sosa is having a party at his mansion tonight," Major Pain said. "We going to crash that bitch," he said with a smile. "Grab a weapon."

Quick looked in the back of one of the vans and saw a range of weapons. He grabbed an AK-47 and three extra clips. He loaded his weapon and stuck the extra clips inside his pocket. Just by looking at each man's face, he could tell that they meant business, that they were looking to impress Turf tonight. He had no idea how the night was going to play out, but one thing he did know; it wasn't going to be pretty.

Five men hopped into each van, as the three vans pulled off, heading toward Sosa's mansion.

"A toast to the good life," Sosa said, and he and Lucky made their glasses touch.

Sosa was happy to have a soldier like Lucky on his team, someone reliable to hold shit down. He had personally seen Lucky put in work, not to mention all the stories circulating in the streets, so he knew the money he was paying Lucky would be well earned.

"Glad to have you on the team."

"Glad to be a part of the team." Lucky smiled. This was too good of an opportunity for him to pass up. Sosa was giving him a chance to make some real money, not nickel-and-dime him like Turf was trying to do.

Lucky, Sosa, and Hawk stood over by the bar area, going over a money scheme that Sosa had up his sleeve. Throughout the mansion, the music was blasting, with women everywhere, most of them barely wearing any clothes. Everybody who was anybody was in the mansion, from rappers to prostitutes, from gold diggers to hustlers who had names for themselves. Even a few athletes were sprinkled throughout the mansion, and everyone seemed to be enjoying themselves.

"This is how we party," Hawk said, looking over at Lucky, who smiled as a Spanish woman slid down onto his lap and began whispering in his ear.

Sosa smiled as he looked around his mansion. He knew that, in this game, any day could be your last, so every chance he got, he treated himself. He told himself life was too short and since he had the money, he might as well use it to his advantage, 'cause once it was over, he wouldn't be able to take any of that money with him. He wanted to enjoy his money, instead of putting some lawyer's whole family through college. Besides, a party never hurt anybody.

Sosa poured himself another glass of Absolut as a nicely shaped white woman with blond hair made her way over into his personal space.

"What you doing over here all by yourself?" she asked with a million-dollar smile.

"Waiting for you." Sosa eyed the woman's curves. "What's your name?" he asked, looking into her blue eyes.

"Kimberly." She had been watching Sosa all night and had patiently awaited a chance to talk to him when he was alone.

"So, what brings you to my party?" Sosa asked, looking over the rim of his glass.

"One of my girlfriends told me about the party," Kimberly told him. "But what she didn't tell me was how fine and sexy you are," she added, openly flirting with the man she had known for less than five minutes.

"Come with me upstairs." Sosa refilled his glass. "I gotta show you something," he said as he led the way upstairs. He reached the top of the steps then walked down the long hallway to the master bedroom.

As soon as the bedroom door closed, Kimberly was all over Sosa. She sloppily kissed his mouth then slowly made her way down to his neck, all the while playing with his dick through his jeans.

Once Kimberly felt what Sosa was working with, she just had to see it up close and in person. She dropped down to her knees and began unbuckling Sosa's belt and pants like she was a fiend. Once she was face-to-face with his pole, she began sucking on it like she owned it, like she needed to taste it to live. She held Sosa's pipe with one hand, while her other hand massaged her own clit. She moaned while sucking all over Sosa's dick, like it was the best thing her taste buds had ever experienced.

Sosa grabbed a handful of Kimberly's blond hair and guided her head to the speed he desired. He looked down at her as he began to stroke her mouth like it was a pussy. The faster he stroked her mouth, the louder she moaned.

After about fifteen minutes of sucking, Sosa wanted to see what Kim's insides felt like. He helped her back up to her feet and ripped her dress off.

Underneath, Kimberly wore no panties. She stood in front of Sosa wearing nothing but a pair of heels.

Sosa rolled on a condom and carried her over toward the bed.

"No, no, no," Kim said. "I want to be on top," she added as she straddled him and began to ride and bounce on Sosa's dick like she was riding a horse.

Sosa lay back and sucked all over Kim's breasts as she continued to bounce up and down.

The three vans pulled onto Sosa's property and parked right on the manicured front lawn. Inside the vans were fifteen men.

About forty to fifty guests stood out front, just enjoying the night air.

"Look at these clowns," Major Pain huffed as he pulled his ski mask down over his face.

The door to the van zipped open, and out jumped five masked men, all holding machine guns. Van number two and number three followed the lead of van number one.

Major Pain set it off. He aimed his AK at the guests who stood out front and squeezed the trigger, waving his arms back and forth, hitting anything moving.

Wolf, Quick, and the rest of the crew ran up inside the mansion, followed by the rest of the soldiers. Inside looked like a packed club; that's how many people filled the mansion.

Quick looked over at Wolf then back at the crowd as he squeezed the trigger. Innocent people dropped like flies, while the others desperately ran for their lives.

Major Pain and the rest of the goons entered the mansion and opened fire.

Lucky was sitting over in the corner entertaining two women when he heard the gunshots erupt throughout the mansion. He quickly went into survival mode, pulling his .45 from his waistband, sending shots toward the entrance of the mansion as he weaved through all the people scrambling for their lives.

He looked over and saw Hawk behind the counter loading up his shotgun.

Hawk sprung from behind the counter and let the shotgun bark. He pumped round after round into the chamber and let it blast.

Lucky took out three of the masked men before his gun went empty. He quickly tossed it to the ground as he ran for the door.

Quick watched bodies drop like flies as he moved deeper inside the mansion. He spotted Lucky making a run for the back exit. He could've easily shot him in the back, but instead, he spared his friend's life as he reloaded his AK and stuck a fresh clip into the base of the gun.

Major Pain walked throughout the mansion making sure everyone downstairs was dead. He stood over a woman who had a hole in her chest. She was gasping for air as she looked up at him. Her eyes screamed, *Please help*.

Major Pain stuck the nose of his AK into the woman's mouth and pulled the trigger.

"Downstairs is clear," he announced as he led the way upstairs.

***

Sosa walked around the room half dressed. The only thing he was missing was his shirt. He poured himself another glass of Absolut. He turned around and saw Kimberly sprawled out across the bed, her heels still on her feet.

"You destroyed my dress," Kimberly said, placing a cigarette inside her mouth. "What am I supposed to wear home?"

Sosa grabbed his shirt from the floor and tossed it at Kim's face. "Here. Put that on and get the fuck out," he said coldly.

"You bastard!" Kimberly spat. "How dare you try and treat me this way!"

Just as Sosa was about to reply, he heard what sounded like gunshots. "Shut the fuck up!" he said to her, holding his finger in the air so he could hear. Seconds later, he heard the sound again. Sosa knew that sound anywhere. Machine guns.

He quickly walked over to his security monitors and turned them on. He looked at the monitors and saw all of his guests scrambling for their lives. He looked at the other monitor and saw Lucky and Hawk returning fire, but they were outnumbered.

"Ay, stay right there!" he said, pointing at Kimberly. He walked over to his gun closet and snatched open the doors. He grabbed the bulletproof vest and strapped it on over his chest. "Bitch-ass niggas wanna run up in my house?" he said to himself as he grabbed the M-16 that rested on the shelf. Then he grabbed four extra clips and shoved them down into his pocket.

"Where's my vest?" Kimberly asked as the gunshots got louder and louder.

Sosa ignored her last comment as he walked back over to the monitors. One of the gunmen had shot out all of the cameras, leaving him looking at a scrambled screen.

"Fuck!" Sosa cursed loudly, trapped inside of a room in a house full of gunmen out looking for his blood. He quickly turned and looked over at Kimberly. "Come here!" he said in a fast-paced voice. "I need you to peek out the door and tell me how close they are."

"Hell no!" Kimberly said, looking at Sosa like he was crazy. "They'll kill me!"

"I'm not going to let them kill you," he said. "All I need you to do is peek your head out the door real quick."

Kim sighed loudly. "Come on, hurry up," she said, and she and Sosa made their way over to the door.

"On the count of three, I want you to just peek your head out the door real quick, and that's it," Sosa told her. "One, two, three!" he quickly snatched open the door, and Kimberly poked her head out the door.

Once Kim's head was out the door, Sosa forcefully shoved her into the hallway and slammed and locked the door behind her. A split second later, he heard at least seven different guns going off, followed by Kimberly's scream.

When the gunshots ended, Sosa snatched open the door with his finger on the trigger of his M-16. He watched the bullets from his gun rip three of the gunmen, while the others scattered like roaches trying not to get hit by one of the bullets, which sounded like thunder. Sosa quickly ducked back inside the room and closed the door as big holes ripped through the door in rapid succession and bullets turned the door into Swiss cheese.

Major Pain stood with his back up against a wall as he watched Quick, Wolf, and the rest of his goons that were still breathing return fire into the door that Sosa had run behind. Major Pain ran toward the door and kicked it open. He stepped inside and saw Sosa hanging out the window, like he was scared to jump. Major Pain aimed his AK at the window and sprayed it, causing Sosa to jump way sooner than he intended.

Sosa landed in the bushes and twisted his ankle. "Ahhh shit!" he growled in pain. At that very moment, he knew his life was about to come to an end.

Out of nowhere, Lucky grabbed Sosa's M-16 from the ground and aimed it up at the window and squeezed the trigger.

Just as Major Pain was about to look out the window to see where Sosa had landed, a loud series of gunshots caused him to get low as he felt a few bullets whistle past his face. With a hand signal, he ordered the rest of his men to head downstairs.

While Lucky held the gunmen at bay, Hawk helped Sosa up to his feet and he hopped on his good leg to the getaway car he had parked out back for situations like this. Lucky held the M-16 up at the window until Hawk swerved around and beeped the horn.

"Come on!" Hawk yelled out the window as he watched Lucky run and hop into the backseat. Hawk put the pedal to the metal as he heard the back window shatter.

Quick watched the car swerve out onto the street as he emptied his clip on the vehicle. He was hoping one of his bullets didn't strike Lucky, but in this game, there were no guarantees.

"Come on, we gotta go!" Major Pain barked, and he and Quick ran through the mansion toward the front door.

By the time they reached the front of the mansion, they saw two of their vans flying down the street. Just as they reached the last van, two cop cars came to a screeching stop, the lights on the top of the cars flashing brightly.

"Get in the van," Major Pain said as he trained his AK at the cop car and held on to the trigger as he swept the gun back and forth.

Quick hopped into the driver's seat of the van as he watched the bullets from Major Pain's AK tear up the two squad cars. Once Major Pain ran out of bullets, he hopped into the passenger seat of the van.

Quick gunned the engine, recklessy pulling out onto the street. He nervously looked through the rearview mirror. "Fuck! We got company," he announced as he saw flashing lights in his rearview.

Major Pain looked over at Quick. "You know what we gotta do," he said, reloading his AK.

Quick nodded his head, signaling that he understood.

Major Pain reached into the backseat and grabbed Quick's AK. He stuck a fresh clip into the gun and set it on Quick's lap.

"Pull over right here," Major Pain said, pointing. "We gotta split up and make a run for it on foot before they call in the helicopter."

Quick stopped the van in the middle of the block as he took a deep breath.

"Meet you back at the spot," Major Pain said.

The two shook hands then hopped out of the van. Quick hopped out first and opened fire on the cop car as he began to backpedal.

Major Pain hopped out, and he, too, opened fire on the cop car until he saw no more movement inside the cop car. He looked over at Quick and nodded his head, and the two men took off running in different directions.

Quick ran down the street with a ski mask covering his face and an AK-47 assault riffle in his hand. He heard pedestrians screaming and moving out of his path. Quick's lungs and heart threatened to burst, but he pressed on, knowing that if he slowed down or got caught, the end result wouldn't be pretty. He turned down a well-lit street, where he dropped his AK on the ground, kicked it under a parked car, and kept walking like nothing had ever happened. Then he rolled his ski mask up so that it looked like a skully on his head.

Quick heard the sirens and quickly dipped into a bar. He walked straight up to the counter and ordered a drink. He looked over both shoulders as he pulled out his cell phone and texted Ivy, telling her to come and pick him up.

She replied, I'm on my way.

Quick sat at the bar and sipped on his drink as he waited for Ivy to arrive.

Major Pain ran down a dark street. The first thing he did was get rid of the AK and the ski mask. He stuck his hand down into his pocket and gripped the .380 that rested there as he walked down the street like he didn't have a care in the world. He made it to the next block and saw flashing lights all over the place and a crowd standing around. He walked over to the crowd. Squeezing through the crowd, he saw Wolf laid out in the middle of the street, his body filled with bullet holes. Three other men also lay dead in the street next to him.

"Fuck!" Major Pain cursed under his breath. He saw Wolf's AK lying right next to him. He knew that if anyone from the crew was stopped by the police, it would be shots fired on sight.

Major Pain saw two police officers laid out dead on the concrete and another officer with a gunshot wound to his leg being helped into the back of an ambulance. He shook his head as he walked off and flagged down a cab.

Major Pain sat in the back of the cab and exhaled loudly. "I hope Quick got away," he thought out loud as he closed his eyes and relaxed for the rest of the ride.

Quick hopped into the passenger side of Ivy's Charger and she pulled off.

"Damn! It's cops all over the place," she said, cruising past a crime scene.

Quick looked out the tinted window in time to see a police officer place a white sheet over Wolf's body.

"Damn! Wolf!" Quick mumbled, and he sat back in silence for the rest of the ride.

When the two got home, Quick removed his clothes and took a quick shower. After he hopped out of the shower, he entered the bedroom and orally pleased Ivy. Once he was done, she quickly drifted off to sleep, while Quick stayed up for most of the night, just staring up at the ceiling.

"Do What You Gotta Do"

Tiffany stepped off the bus and couldn't wait to get home and out of the cold. She had a long day at work and just wanted to go home and relax. Surprisingly, for the past week, Blake had been acting normal, not like a jackass. Tiffany was just hoping that this pattern continued. She reached the lobby and repeatedly pressed the call button for the elevator. She stepped inside and pressed her floor, rubbing her hands together in an attempt to warm them up.

Tiffany stepped off the elevator and saw a woman exiting her apartment. When she looked closely, she realized it was the same girl from the last time.

"Hold that elevator," the mystery woman said, her heels click-clacking loudly on the floor as she jogged toward the elevator.

Tiffany stood in the doorway of the elevator so it wouldn't close. "Can I talk to you for a second?"

The mystery woman looked her up and down and replied, "Nah. I don't have nothing to say to you. Besides, I don't know you."

"Well, you gon' tell me something," Tiffany said, her voice rising. "This is the second time I caught you coming out of my house."

"Your house?" the mystery woman echoed, a smirk on her face.

Just from that smirk, Tiffany knew that Blake had been telling the woman all kinds of lies. "Were you in my house having sex with my boyfriend?" Tiffany asked. She pulled three twenty-dollar bills from her pocket and held them out toward the woman.

The woman took the money and stuck it down into her bra. "Who? Blake?" she said, loudly popping her gum.

"Yes, Blake."

"Yeah, he's one of my best customers," the woman told her. "And a good tipper."

"So that's what he does with my hard-earned money," Tiffany said to herself as she stepped back and let the elevator door close. She couldn't believe what she had just heard, even though she had already expected it.

Tiffany slowly made her way down the hallway and entered her apartment. She stepped inside the house and looked at Blake with a disgusted look on her face.

"Hey, baby," Blake said, sitting back on the couch, a gun resting in front of him on the coffee table.

Tiffany didn't even respond to Blake. She walked past him like he was invisible and went into the bedroom and slammed the door.

Seconds later, Blake came bursting into the room. "What the fuck is your problem?" he barked, grabbing Tiffany under her chin and forcing her to look at him.

"Fuck you!" Tiffany capped back, smacking Blake's hand off her face.

She was instantly smacked down to the floor. Then a kick to her ribs came next, followed by Blake snatching her back up to her feet by her hair. "Bitch, what the fuck is your problem?"

"Why don't you go ask that prostitute bitch that you been giving all of my money to!" Tiffany huffed as she grabbed a duffel bag from the closet and began filling it with her clothes.

"Fuck you think you going?" Blake asked, fire dancing in his eyes.

"Fuck you! I'm sick of you and all of your shit!"

"Put that bag down before I get angry," Blake warned, his nostrils flared and his hands turned to fists.

"Hmm!" Tiffany sighed loudly, ignoring Blake's last comment.

"I'm not playing with you!"

Out of all nights, tonight was one of those nights that Blake didn't want to fight with Tiffany. At the moment, he had bigger and more important things on his mind. He had just purchased a new gun and planned on going out the following day to look for Quick. He was going to put him in his place for butting into his business that day at the restaurant.

"Do what you gotta do," Tiffany spat, her tone showing no respect as she continued to pack her things.

Blake slowly walked up to her, and she dropped her bag and took a defensive stance. No longer was she going to stand around and just let him pound on her. Those days were over.

When Blake got a little too close to Tiffany, she popped her arm out and punched him in the eye. "You better back up!" she said, ready for battle.

Blake held his eye and smiled. This was the first time Tiffany had ever hit him. Usually, he was the one doing the hitting.

He quickly rushed Tiffany, scooped her legs up, and slammed her down to the floor like she was a rag doll. "Have you lost your muthafuckin' mind?" he growled, raining punches on her exposed face.

Tiffany's face was a bloody mess, but that didn't stop Blake from beating her ass like she was a man. He continued to hit her with forceful blow after forceful blow.

Once his arms got tired, he stood to his feet and started stomping her.

Tiffany's face was still cold from just coming inside the house, which only made Blake's boots feel like stone hitting her all across her body. The only thing Tiffany could do was ball up and wildly kick her legs, all the while screaming at the top of her lungs.

"Say you sorry!" Blake barked, kicking her one more time.

"I'm sorry."

Blake kicked her in the face. "You sorry, what?"

"I'm sorry, Daddy." Tiffany coughed up blood.

Tiffany had never been in this much pain in her life. This time, Blake had really beat the shit out of her. Her mind quickly raced to the knife that she'd hidden in her drawer. Her eyes then locked on the gun resting on the coffee table.

"Now get over here and suck this dick!" Blake huffed. He pulled out his dick and put it in Tiffany's bloody face. "I keep telling you, you belong to me, bitch!"

"I can't," Tiffany told him. "Both of my lips are swollen." She spat blood onto the floor.

Blake looked down and examined her puffy lips. "Get over here!" he said. He began to jerk his dick, while Tiffany stayed on her knees.

Blake grunted as he came and exploded all over Tiffany's face. "You belong to me, and you ain't going no muthafuckin' where!"

Blake sat back on the couch and propped his feet up on the coffee table. "Now get out of my sight," he said, fanning his hand.

Tiffany got up off her knees and went to the bathroom. She looked in the mirror and saw her face covered with blood and semen. She grabbed her rag, wet it, and cleaned her face. She took a deep breath before turning on the shower and heading to the bedroom.

She opened her drawer and removed the shiny knife and held it down at her side as she slowly walked back to the living room. She stood directly behind Blake with the knife in her hand as she watched him laugh at an episode of *Martin*, like nothing had just happened. Just the sight of Blake made her angry and want to kill.

Just as she was about to stab him, she started thinking, *What if I kill him? Then I'ma get put in jail for the rest of my life. What if he don't die, then disarms me and kills me?*

Then she remembered what her face just looked like in the mirror. "Fuck you!" Tiffany screamed as she raised the knife and brought it down with all of her might, stabbing Blake in his chest.

Tiffany stabbed Blake repeatedly, until his body stopped moving. "Muthafucka!" she growled as she dropped the knife onto the floor. She ran to the back room and grabbed her pocketbook. Then she ran to the front door full speed before she suddenly stopped dead in her tracks.

She quickly ran back and picked up the knife from the floor and tossed it inside her pocketbook. Tiffany made it to the hallway, running full speed, then disappeared down the staircase.

Just as Tiffany disappeared down the staircase, two cops stepped off the elevator. One of the neighbors had called the cops and reported a domestic disturbance.

Tiffany made it outside and ran straight for the subway. She was hoping that her mother was home, because she didn't have a key to her mother's house.

She stepped onto the train and could feel the other passengers staring at her. She just stared down at the floor until she arrived at her stop.

It was so cold outside, especially since she'd left her coat back at the house. Tiffany jogged from the train station to her mother's house, where she knocked on the door and patiently awaited an answer.

Brenda snatched open the door and was about to start talking shit, until she saw her daughter's swollen face. "Oh my God! Get in here," she said, rushing Tiffany inside the apartment.

"What You Gonna Do?"

Quick woke up to something wet on his penis. He opened his eyes and saw Ivy's head bobbing up and down.

He smiled as he rested his arms behind his head and stared up at the ceiling. Just a few weeks ago, he didn't know what he was going to do with his life. Today, he was waking up to some porno head. Quick's future looked bright. He didn't want to be a drug dealer forever, so he planned on just using the drug business as a stepping-stone. His dream was to be a legitimate business owner, and he didn't plan on letting anything stop him from reaching his goal.

Once Quick exploded, Ivy got up and headed to the bathroom to take a shower. Quick threw on his sweat pants as he made his way to the kitchen and grabbed the box of Frosted Flakes from the top of the refrigerator.

Bang! And his front door flew open.

Quick nervously dropped the box of Frosted Flakes to the floor when he saw Lucky standing in his living room with a .45 aimed at his head.

"Yo, what is you doing?" Quick asked with his hands up in the air in surrender.

"Were you with those niggas that Turf sent to Sosa's house the other night?" Lucky asked. His voice held a serious tone, his .45 aimed at Quick's head.

"Nah," Quick lied. "I heard about it though. I tried to give you the heads-up, but your phone kept going to voice mail that day."

Lucky thought back, and he remembered his phone dying that day and not being able to find his charger to save his life. He slowly lowered his weapon.

"Why did you just jump ship like that and go deal with Sosa?" Quick asked.

"Sosa not trying to spoon-feed me," Lucky answered quickly. "He's giving me a chance to make some real money and do less work. I told him about you, and he sent me down here to make you a offer." Lucky paused. "Whatever Turf is paying you, he's willing to triple that."

"C'mon, you know I'm a loyal nigga."

"You loyal to Turf?" Lucky asked, his face screwed up. "That nigga don't give a fuck about neither one of us, and you know it."

"I know, but I already"—Quick turned when, out of the corner of his eye, he saw Ivy appear, wrapped in a towel.

The sight caught Lucky off guard, and he raised his gun and pulled the trigger.

POW!

"Oh shit!" Lucky said when he recognized the woman as Quick's new girlfriend. "I—I'm sorry. She came out of nowhere."

Quick ran toward Ivy and kneeled next to her body. He pulled out his cell phone and dialed 9-1-1.

"Hang in there, baby," he said as he held on to Ivy's hand. "You going to be fine, baby. Hang in there," he said, looking at the blood oozing out of the small hole in her stomach.

"I'm sorry. It was a accident, Quick. You know that was a accident, right?"

Quick ignored his friend's comments as he watched the life bleed out of the one woman he ever had real feelings for.

Ivy gave Quick a bloody smile. "I love you, baby," she whispered weakly.

"It was a accident, Quick," Lucky said as he heard sirens in the distance. "It was a accident," he said again as he backpedaled out the front door.

Quick stayed at Ivy's side as he watched her lifeless eyes drift off into space. A tear escaped his eye as he took his two fingers and closed her eyes.

Seconds later, Ivy's apartment was full of cops and paramedics.

Quick found himself answering questions all night. The cops placed a sheet over Ivy's body and left her lying right there on the floor where she'd died after they took pictures of her and the entire apartment.

Detective Davis stepped out of his car and flicked his cigarette into the street. He had been up for the past four nights, going over details of two different cases. He walked inside the apartment and looked at the murder scene.

"What do we have here?" he asked a uniformed officer.

The uniformed officer told him, "Twenty-seven-year-old woman dead. Seems as if someone kicked the door in and shot her."

"Was anything stolen?" Detective Davis asked as he pulled out his pen and notepad.

"Nope," the uniformed officer answered. "I think it was drug-related though, because her boyfriend was here, but he's not talking."

"Boyfriend?" Detective Davis echoed, a smirk on his face.

"Yeah, he's right over there." The uniformed officer pointed over in Quick's direction.

Detective Davis looked over in the direction the officer pointed and saw Quick sitting over in the corner with tears in his eyes. "Oh shit! That's the new guy," he said to himself. He remembered seeing Quick's face as he left the trap house the other day.

Detective Davis walked up to Quick and pulled out a pack of cigarettes. "Cigarette?"

"No, thank you," Quick said, his mind all over the place at the moment. He thought about killing Lucky. The only thing saving him was the fact that it was an accident.

"Care to tell me what happened here today?" Detective Davis asked.

"I've answered these questions a thousand times already," Quick said.

"Well, now you going to answer them a thousand and one times," Detective Davis said, matching Quick's tone.

"Me and my girl was in here chilling," Quick began. "Next thing I know, I heard a loud boom, followed by the door getting busted open."

"Then what happened?"

"I remembered Ivy was in the shower. When I hopped out the bed, I heard a single shot. By the time I made it to the living room, I saw her laid out on the floor, bleeding."

"So you didn't see the man or men who done this?" Detective Davis asked with a raised brow.

"No."

"Did Ivy have any enemies or anyone who might want to see her dead?" Detective Davis asked.

"Not that I know of," Quick told him with a straight face.

The detective pressed, "Do you have any enemies that may've killed her to get to you?"

"Nope," Quick replied.

Detective Davis knew he was wasting his time. Quick wasn't going to talk, and he knew it. He never could understand the stupid street code of silence. Why wouldn't a man help the police put away the person who had just killed his girlfriend, especially if he had information that could help?

Quick sat answering questions for most of the day, until the cops and detectives finally left. Even after five hours of questioning, he kept telling the same story over and over again. "I don't know who could've done this."

After having the cops fucking with him all day, Quick stepped out of the house and hopped into his car and decided to just go for a ride. His mind was so scrambled and all over the place, he didn't even notice Detective Davis tailing him.

The first stop Quick made was at the liquor store. He hopped out the whip and disappeared inside the store. Minutes later, he returned, carrying a bottle of Cîroc. He cracked the bottle open and guzzled straight from it as he pulled back out into traffic. He still couldn't believe what had just happened. Half of him wanted to hate Lucky, but the other half wouldn't let him.

Quick thought long and hard as he cruised the city getting drunk. He wanted to kill Lucky, but how could he come to kill the same person he had grown up with?

Before Quick knew it, his bottle was halfway empty. "Fuck!" he cursed loudly as he felt his stomach began to feel a little nauseated. He realized he hadn't eaten anything all day.

"Fuck it!" Quick said, pulling inside the IHOP parking lot. He cut the engine off and walked toward the entrance. As he was walking in, a customer coming out bumped into him. He nodded his head and quickly apologized for being in the way.

Quick followed the hostess over to a booth over in the corner. He rested his head on the table for a second, trying to get his thoughts together. His head was spinning, along with a million thoughts on his mind.

"Hey," Tiffany said, knocking on the top of the table to get Quick's attention. "You all right?" she asked, her voice full of concern.

Quick looked up and saw Tiffany's bruised-up face. "Yeah, I'm fine. Can I have some water, please?"

"Yeah, sure," Tiffany said, and she went to go get Quick some water. She returned with a glass of water and two aspirin. "Here you go." She set the glass of water down on the table. "I brought you some aspirin too."

Quick tossed the two pills into his mouth and washed it down with some water. "What happened to your face?" he asked. Instantly, he could see the embarrassment on her face.

"I'm okay," Tiffany said, not knowing what else to say. She knew sooner or later, somebody else besides her mother was going to ask her about the bruises that she'd tried to cover up with too much makeup.

"Well, you don't look okay to me." Quick checked out her bruises. He knew Blake had to be responsible.

"And neither do you," Tiffany shot back.

Before Quick could say another word, two detectives and three uniformed officers came storming up into the restaurant. Immediately, Quick's heart sank into his stomach. He knew the cops were going to try and make it seem like he had something to do with Ivy's murder.

One of the detectives shouted, "You're under arrest!" as he forcefully slammed Tiffany face-first onto Quick's table and slapped the cuffs on her.

"Under arrest for what?" Tiffany asked, wincing in pain.

"Attempted murder!" The detective snatched Tiffany up and escorted her out of the restaurant.

Tiffany and Quick made eye contact as the officers escorted her out of her place of work. Quick looked on with the rest of the diners as the detectives roughly tossed her into the back of the unmarked car before pulling off.

Tiffany sat in the back of the detective car, tears streaming down her face. She knew it was only a matter of time before the cops came for her. All of her things were still inside the house, along with pictures of her and Blake together. Everything had happened so fast. She hadn't had time to remove all traces of her being or living there.

"I feel sorry for you." The detective shook his head as he looked at Tiffany through the rearview mirror. "Them butch bitches are going to love you," he said, taunting her. "With that nice ass you got, they gon' pass you around like a cigarette." He laughed.

If looks could kill, the detective's head would've been cut off. Tiffany did her best to tune out the detective. She continued to remain silent as they pulled up to the station.

When Tiffany got inside, the detective placed her in a holding cell along with a few other women.

"Fuck!" Tiffany cursed as she sat down on the wooden bench and leaned her head back against the wall. For a second, she just thought about how her life had slowly gone down the drain. "It wasn't supposed to be like this," she said to herself.

She thought about how the next few years in jail would be, and she began to cry again. "Get yourself together," Tiffany told herself as she wiped her face. "Fuck it! If this is where I have to stay for the next ten years, so be it." She figured being in jail was better than living with Blake.

After Tiffany sat in the cold cell for two hours, the detective finally came and called her name. She stepped out of the cell and followed the detective to the interrogation room.

“Cigarette?” the detective asked, holding the pack out to her.

“I’m good,” Tiffany said as she sat back in the chair.

“So,” the detective began, “why did you try to kill your boyfriend, Blake Robinson?”

“I don’t know what you talking about. I don’t even have a boyfriend.”

“Bullshit!” the detective yelled. “Your clothes, toothbrush, and pictures of you were found all throughout the apartment.”

“And?”

“And I think you have some explaining to do.” The detective placed a pen and pad in front of her.

“I stopped dealing with Blake months ago. I moved back in with my moms for a few months, and she’ll tell you the same thing.”

The detective laughed. “That’s funny, because I just spoke to Blake, and he told me that you were the one who had stabbed him,” he lied, trying to come at Tiffany from a different angle, hoping that she would fold.

Tiffany swallowed hard but remained quiet and just listened. She knew that if the detective knew what he needed to know, he wouldn’t be questioning her right now.

"And our friend Blake is prepared to press charges against you," the detective said, continuing to lie. "You looking at fifteen years minimum."

Tiffany just remained quiet as she listened to what the detective had to say. After two hours of listening to that bullshit, she was taken back to the cell, where she waited a few more hours until it was time for her to see a judge.

Tiffany almost passed out when she heard the judge set her bail at $200,000. After the court officer escorted her back to her holding cell, all she could do was wait and see what the next step in the process was.

Two hours later, a CO called her name.

"Get your shit. You just made bail," he announced as he led her toward the front desk to fill out her paperwork.

This has to be some kind of mistake, she thought to herself as she nervously filled out her release papers. She knew nobody in her family even had close to one hundred dollars, let alone twenty thousand. She filled out the papers and quickly walked out of the station before they realized that the system was making a mistake.

When Tiffany stepped outside, she saw Quick leaning on the hood of a Dodge Charger. "You bailed me out?" she asked, walking up to him.

"Yeah," Quick answered as he walked around to the driver's side of the car and hopped in.

Tiffany followed his lead and slid into the passenger seat. "Why did you bail me out?"

"Jail ain't no place for no one," Quick said, pulling away from the curb.

"I appreciate it, but I can't afford to pay you back."

"I didn't ask you to pay me back," Quick said as the sound of Jay-Z hummed through the speakers at a low level. "What's going on with you and that nigga Blake?"

"Nothing," Tiffany answered quickly. "I tried to kill his ass. That's why the cops came to get me."

"You shot him?"

"No. Stabbed him up." Tiffany wasn't proud of what she had done, but she just felt she did what she had to do.

Quick smirked. "Damn! I guess I better stay on your good side." He laughed out loud.

"Where are you taking me?"

"Wherever you want to go," Quick answered. "Where do you live?"

"Live?" Tiffany laughed. "Wherever I can at the moment, until I get my shit together."

"I just got a new apartment. You're welcome to stay there with me, if you like."

"I don't know," Tiffany said, putting up a weak protest. "You've already done too much for me, don't you think?"

"Trust me, you won't even know I'm there when I am there, 'cause most of the time, I'm out."

"Okay, I'll stay with you until I get back on my feet. Deal?"

"Deal," Quick said, and the two shook hands.

Thirty minutes later, Quick pulled up in front of his new apartment and shut off the engine. "Sorry, but I don't have any furniture yet." He popped the trunk and removed a box containing an air mattress. "I hope you don't mind sleeping on this," he said, holding up the box.

"No. That will be perfectly fine," Tiffany said with a smile as the two stepped inside the empty apartment.

Immediately, Quick plugged in the air pump and blew up the bed. Then he went and grabbed some sheets and made the bed.

"I have to step out for a few. You need anything?"

"Just some sleep," Tiffany said, lying down on the air mattress.

Just as Quick was about to head out the door, she called his name, stopping him dead in his tracks.

"Thank you for everything."

Quick smiled and winked as he headed out the door. He hopped back into his car and headed down toward the church.

When Quick pulled up to the back of the church, he saw Turf and Goliath coming out the back door.

"Look at this nigga," Turf said with a smirk on his face. "Glad to see you still alive."

"Glad to still be alive." Quick smiled. "I saw the police got to Wolf. Did Major Pain make out all right?"

"Yeah, he's fine," Turf said, as he and Goliath slid into the awaiting Range Rover. The passenger window immediately rolled down. "This spot is dead from now on," Turf added. "I'll have Goliath text you the new meeting spot tomorrow. Go home and get you some rest," he said, and the Range Rover pulled off.

"I like how that kid moves," Turf said to Goliath. He could tell that Quick was hungry, and on top of that, he was loyal. Turf also liked the fact that Quick used his head before he reacted. That was something that couldn't be taught. Either you had it, or you didn't. A few more months up under Turf's wing, and Quick was going to be heading toward the top fast.

"We got some company," Goliath said when he noticed flashing lights in his rearview mirror.

"Pull this muthafucka over," Turf said in a calm voice. He removed his P89 from his waistband and handed it to Goliath, who placed both Turf's gun and his own gun inside the secret compartment in the dashboard.

Goliath pulled over and placed the Range Rover in park. He watched the cop's every move from his side mirror.

"He fuckin' with us for no reason. I ain't did shit wrong," Goliath said as the detective made his way to the driver's window.

Detective Davis tapped on the driver's window with his flashlight. "Roll this muthafucka down," he ordered, shining the bright light directly in Goliath's eyes.

"What seems to be the problem?" Goliath asked, an angry look on his face. If the man standing in front of his window wasn't a cop, he would've gladly killed the man with his bare hands.

"I'll ask the questions around here," Detective Davis told the giant who sat behind the wheel. "License and registration." He watched the big man reach over to the glove compartment and remove the items he had requested.

"Here you go, sir." Goliath handed him his license and registration, and through his side mirror, he watched the detective walk back to his car.

Goliath huffed, anger all in his tone. “Bitch-ass nigga fuckin’ with us for no reason.”

“Just be cool. We clean, so he can’t do shit to us anyway,” Turf said calmly. He was already used to the harassment by the police; it was all a part of the game. You had to take the bad along with the good, and to be the boss, you definitely had to pay the cost.

Detective Davis walked back up to the driver’s window and tossed Goliath’s license and paperwork at him. “I want you two drug-dealing scumbags to stay the fuck off my streets!” he spat. “The next time I catch you two punk muthafuckas on my streets, I’ma make sure y’all have hell to pay.” Detective Davis looked over at Turf and saw a smirk on his face. “Something funny?”

“Only thing funny I see is you,” Turf shot back.

“Tough guy, huh?” Detective Davis smiled as he walked to the passenger side of the Range Rover. He called for backup right before he reached the passenger side window. “You got a problem over here, boy?”

“The problem is, you fuckin’ with us for no reason,” Turf replied. “You ain’t got nothing else better to do with your life?”

Turf and Goliath burst out laughing.

"Tell you what," Turf said, looking in the detective's eyes. "When you ready to stop working for the man and start working for a real man, holla at me, and I might give you a job."

"You a funny muthafucka." Detective Davis laughed as he noticed his backup pulling up to the scene. "Step out the car."

"For what?" Turf asked.

"I said step out the car!" Detective Davis yelled as he opened the passenger side door and snatched Turf out of the passenger seat.

Turf's feet hit the pavement, and from there on out, it was on. He turned and punched the detective in his face as the two broke out into a scuffle right on the side of the road.

The other officer quickly ran over and jumped into the brawl, striking Turf repeatedly with his nightstick.

Goliath hopped out of the driver's seat and laid the officer out with one punch. Then he made his way over to Detective Davis and wrapped his hands around his neck and applied pressure.

"Look at you now, muthafucka," Turf said as he punched the detective in his face.

Detective Davis tried his best to pry the big man's hands from around his throat, but it was no use. Goliath's grip was too deadly.

When Turf saw Detective Davis's eyes start to roll into the back of his head, he stepped in. "That's enough," he said, and immediately, Goliath let go of the detective's neck.

Detective Davis's body hit the ground, and Turf and Goliath busted out laughing.

Seconds later, cop cars swarmed the area. Turf and Goliath lay down on the ground in surrender. They knew the NYPD was going to put a beating on them, but they definitely didn't plan on going out without a fight.

"Shit Is Fucked Up"

Sosa hopped into the awaiting limousine with his lawyer, Mr. Goldberg, by his side. Inside the limo sat Lucky and Hawk.

The first thing Sosa did was pour himself a glass of straight vodka. He took a sip. "What it's looking like?" he said, looking over at his lawyer. He knew he was in some deep shit and might end up doing some jail time.

"Well, the cops say they just want to question you, but they are going to arrest you once you get there," Mr. Goldberg told him. "I called the police station and told them you were on your way." Then he added, "You going missing for a week doesn't make it look too good."

"Fuck they want me to do?" Sosa huffed. "Go running to go sit up in a jail cell? Fuck outta here! Them crackers can kiss my ass!"

"The house that the shooting took place in is not in your name; therefore, you are responsible for what took place in there," Mr. Goldberg told him straight up. He knew that wasn't what Sosa wanted to hear, but he was always straight up with his clients, whether they liked it or not. "We can't even come up with a story, because they have a few witnesses who were at the party, who place you not only at the party, but also as being the host."

Sosa just sipped on his drink as he continued to listen to what his lawyer was telling him. From what he was hearing, it looked like jail time was definitely going to be in his future.

"If these muthafuckas talking about giving me a lot of time, then I'm just going to bail out and take my chances on the run. Fuck it!" He shrugged.

"A lot of people got killed inside of your home, and the DA is going to try to make you responsible for all of them. They can't do that, but they damn sure are going to try."

"So what do you think I should do?" Sosa asked, leaning back in his seat. "Or, better yet, how much is it going to cost to make this go away?"

"It's not that simple. Either you're going to fight it, or you're going to run."

Sosa sat back and started to think about his future. He was willing to take anything under five years. Anything more than that, and he was just going to be on the run. He knew the DA was going to try and make him look like some heartless animal, but he didn't care.

"Fuck it! It is what it is," Sosa said out loud. He didn't have time to just be sitting around and worrying about this shit all day.

The limousine pulled up in front of the police station, and there were people and reporters all over the place, waiting for Sosa to turn himself in.

Sosa looked over at Lucky and Hawk. "This shit ain't over. I want y'all to go pay that punk muthafucka Turf a visit." Then he said to Lucky, "I like how you took out your homeboy's girlfriend. If he ain't with us, then he's against us."

"That shit was an accident. I didn't mean to kill that girl."

"Ain't no such thing as an accident when it comes to murder." Sosa finished his drink. "Y'all hold it down for me while I'm up in here," he said as he and his lawyer hopped out of the limo and faced the large crowd.

Two police officers pushed their way through the large crowd of people and grabbed Sosa's arms.

As Sosa made his way through the crowd, he heard a few people supporting him, a few people hating, and some chanting racial slurs. He ignored all as he made his way inside the police station.

***

Blake woke up in the hospital, not knowing where he was. The last thing he could remember was Tiffany getting fly at the mouth with him, and him putting her in her place.

He tried to move his arm. That's when he quickly found out he was handcuffed to the bed. "What the fuck?" he said out loud. His mouth was dry, and his tongue felt like sandpaper. He desperately needed a drink of water.

"Nurse!" he yelled. He didn't know what was going on, but he was about to get some answers from somewhere. "Nurse!" he called again.

"Stop all that muthafuckin' yelling!" Detective Davis said, stepping inside of Blake's room.

"Why am I handcuffed?" Blake asked, panic in his voice.

Detective Davis furrowed his brow. "Maybe because you're under arrest."

"For what?" Blake barked. "I'm the one laying up in the fuckin' hospital."

"For possession of a firearm." Detective Davis smiled. "I should be taking your ass to jail for beating on that poor girlfriend of yours," he said, standing over Blake. "While you're sitting up in jail, I hope them big, strong muthafuckas beat you up every day the way you did that poor girl."

"I don't know what you talking about," Blake said, feigning ignorance. "I'm a ladies' man. I don't have no reason to hit a woman."

"Hmm." Detective Davis huffed. "That's bullshit. You been whipping that girl's ass, and she finally got tired of it and stabbed your dumb ass. Don't lie to me. I saw the bruises on the poor girl's face."

"Whatever."

Detective Davis smiled. "I'll be back next week, when you're a little better, to tell you where you'll be going for the next three and a half years." He shook his head. "I hope they don't beat on you like you a woman." Detective Davis walked out of the room laughing.

"Bitch-ass nigga," Blake mumbled as he watched the detective stroll out of the room. He was pissed. Not only was he lying up in a hospital bed in pain, but now he'd just found out that the next three and a half years of his life would be spent in a cell.

He wasn't too much worried about the jail time. He was more angry that Tiffany had stabbed him and tried to take his life. If she hadn't stabbed him, he wouldn't be laid up in the hospital, nor would he be on his way to jail. The more he thought about the situation, the more he thought about killing her. He was definitely going to make her pay for the chaos she had caused, just by being defiant.

He said to himself, "As good as I was to that bitch . . . and she gon' do me like this?" Ways to hurt Tiffany flowed through his mind. She had won this round, but he was definitely in it for twelve rounds.

After the officers finished fucking Turf and Goliath up for putting their hands on Detective Davis and the other officer, they tossed them into different holding cells. Turf wiped his bloody nose with the bottom of his shirt. He needed to sit down for a second, but when he looked up, he saw that both benches were full with other inmates.

He walked up to the end of the bench and snatched up the last man sitting down. "Get the fuck up!" he barked, roughly shoving the man to the middle of the cell. The man popped shit, but he didn't do anything but have a seat on the floor.

"Fuck!" Turf yelled loudly, drawing crazy stares from the rest of the inmates. His body was in tremendous pain, and he so badly wanted to kill each and every one of the officers who'd helped partake in his ass whipping.

He spat blood on the floor. Then he closed his eyes and rested his head back against the wall, waiting for one of his women to come and bail him out.

Turf rested his eyes until he heard the cell door open. He opened one eye and saw a CO shove Sosa inside the cell. At first, he thought he was dreaming, until he saw Sosa sitting over at the end of the bench.

Turf immediately stood to his feet, and the two men met in the middle of the cell and, without thinking twice, went blow for blow right there. The other inmates yelled and chanted as they watched the action-packed fight.

Sosa and Turf went at it like two professional fighters, neither man backing down, each one taking it just as good as they gave it. The fight spilled over to the back of the cell by the toilet. The more the two fought, the louder the other inmates became.

Seconds later, several COs ran into the cell and broke up the fight. The officers placed Turf and Sosa into two different cells.

"Put that bitch in here with me!" Goliath yelled as he clung to the bars, watching the officer escort Sosa to the cell directly across from him. "I'ma kill you when I catch you, muthafucka."

"You ain't gon' do shit!" Sosa yelled back. "Better hope I don't catch y'all on the streets."

"You a dead man walking!" Goliath yelled, wishing he could get ahold of Sosa and rip him apart.

"You on borrowed time, muthafucka!" Sosa huffed as he walked over and took a seat on the bench and waited until it was time for him to see the judge.

Lucky and Hawk stormed up into the church with about fifteen goons behind them. The looks on their faces said they meant business. Before Lucky could make his way up the steps to where Turf usually held his meetings, the pastor stopped him.

"Can I help you gentlemen with something?" the pastor asked humbly.

"Yeah, you actually can," Lucky said, and he quickly stole on the pastor, knocking him out with one punch. He and Hawk then quickly pulled out their weapons as they made their way up the steps.

Lucky kicked open the door and he, Hawk, and the rest of the crew busted inside the room. "Fuck!" Lucky saw that the room was completely empty. He figured Turf would move his meeting spot once he'd sent his goons out to try to kill Sosa.

Lucky was no dummy, so he knew that, more than likely, Turf would switch up spots. Until they found out where Turf and his crew had relocated, he would just have to be patient.

"Come on, let's be out," Lucky said, leading the pack out of the church the same way they had come in.

Lucky watched as the rest of the goons hopped back into the van they'd rode in. A few members from the church came outside to see who had assaulted their pastor. They yelled angry words, but nobody did anything.

Lucky rudely spat on the ground just before he hopped into the passenger side of the Lexus that awaited him. The Lexus pulled out of the church's parking lot and bent the corner to the sound of Fabolous pumping through the car's speakers.

"You know Sosa going to have to do time, right?" Hawk said, keeping his eyes on the road as he spoke.

"You think so?" Lucky replied.

"More than likely. So that means me and you going to be the ones running the empire now," Hawk told him. "You up for that?"

"You already know."

Lucky was born to be a boss but could be a soldier if need be, or whatever, to get the job done. With the information Hawk had just laid on him, he knew that, soon, the big bucks would come rolling in. But he also knew more money just meant bigger decisions to be made.

"We going to play this shit by ear," Hawk said as the two continued to cruise the city.

“Living”

After begging Mr. Richardson for another chance, Tiffany was allowed her job back, as long as she could promise that her crazy boyfriend, Blake, wouldn’t pop up at her job anymore, starting shit.

Tiffany worked the day stress free, and did it with a smile on her face. This smile was a natural one, not the usual forced one to cover the pain that she hid inside.

At the end of the night, she counted up her tips, grabbed her coat, then clocked out after saying her good-byes. She exited the restaurant. “Damn!” she huffed as the cold air slapped her in her face as soon as she stepped outside.

While walking, she heard someone yell out, “Yooooo.”

She turned around and saw Quick sitting on the hood of the Charger. She’d only recognized him by the car, because the hoodie he wore covered half of his face.

"What you doing out here?" she said, sliding into Quick's arm, giving him a quick hug.

"Waiting for you to get off," Quick said. "Thought you could use a ride."

"Thanks."

Tiffany hopped into the passenger seat of the car, out of the cold, and Quick sped out of the parking lot and out into the street. They cruised as the sound of Ne-Yo hummed softly through the speakers.

As Quick drove, he peeked over at Tiffany every now and then, just to make sure she was all right.

"What's wrong?" Tiffany asked, catching him peeking at her.

"You was so quiet over there, I just wanted to make sure you was still alive." He laughed.

"I'm good," Tiffany said. "I was just thinking."

"About?" Quick asked, taking his eyes off the road for a second to look at her.

"I mean, why are you being so nice to me? Is it something that you want from me?"

Quick laughed for a second. "Why is it that I must want something from you? 'Cause I'm being nice to you?"

"I'm just saying," she said, turning to face him, "you letting me stay at your house and everything, you ain't charging me no rent or nothing. I just wanna know what's up."

"You looked like you needed a little help, that's all. I don't want nothing from you."

Quick parked in front of his apartment and shut the engine off, and he and Tiffany entered the apartment. Tiffany disappeared into the bathroom, so she could take a shower.

Quick walked over to the kitchen and helped himself to a drink as he read a text message from Major Pain that read, Be at your crib in 30 min. Be ready to roll out.

Quick slid his phone back into its case and downed the liquid fire in one gulp. Seconds later, Tiffany stepped out of the shower covered in a towel.

"My bad," Quick apologized as he headed back toward the bedroom and waited for Major Pain to arrive.

The bedroom, where Quick kept all of his money, was off-limits to Tiffany. He pulled a stack out of his pocket, quickly counted it, then tossed it into the bag with the rest of his money. Seconds later, Quick heard somebody outside beeping the horn like a madman. He shook his head, knowing it could only be Major Pain.

"Yo, I'll be back in a few," he said as he flew out the door.

He stepped out of his apartment and saw the black Escalade waiting curbside. He opened the passenger door, and the loud sound of Dipset's new mixtape came blasting out.

"What's good, my G?" Quick said, and the two men slapped hands.

"Glad to see you still alive," Major Pain said, pulling away from the curb. "Gotta go pick Turf and Goliath up from jail."

"Jail?" Quick repeated. "What they doing in jail?"

"Heard they got it on wit' some Ds," Major Pain told him, weaving his way through traffic with his gun resting on his lap. He always seemed to be ready for action.

"Fucked up what happened to that nigga Wolf."

"Yeah," Major Pain said. "That was my nigga. I put in a lot of work with that man and saw him put in a lot of work. God rest his soul."

Major Pain pulled up in front of the jail and patiently waited. "I heard Sosa and his team bum-rushed your girl's crib and smoked her," he said, looking over at Quick, waiting for him to confirm the story.

"Yeah, it's true," Quick said, thinking back on Ivy. He couldn't express what he felt for her, how real she was, her natural beauty. Ivy was definitely irreplaceable, but like it or not, he had to move on with his life. Even though she was gone, he would still hold a special place in his heart for her, no matter what.

"Tomorrow, we gotta go take care of some high-class Italian club owner," Major Pain said, his eyes glued to the front of the police station.

"Not a problem," Quick said, as if snatching a human life was no big deal.

Quick heard his cell phone ringing. He glanced down at the caller ID and saw Kat's name flashing across the screen. He immediately sent her straight to voice mail as he continued his conversation.

"What time we gotta do that tomorrow?"

"Not sure, but early though." Major Pain saw Turf and Goliath strolling out of the police station. He tapped the horn twice, catching the attention of the two men.

Turf and Goliath slid into the backseat.

"Get me away from this fuckin' place!" Turf couldn't stand the sight of the station any longer.

"What happened with you and Sosa back there?" Goliath asked.

"What?" Major Pain looked at Turf through the rearview mirror. "That nigga Sosa was up in there with y'all?"

"Yeah," Turf said, leaning back in his seat. "That nigga walked up in there like he was the man. When he saw me, he almost shit himself." He decided to embellish the story a little.

As Quick listened to the story, he heard his cell phone ringing again. Again, he saw Kat's name flashing across the screen, and once again, he sent her straight to voice mail.

"As soon as that nigga touch down, he's dead," Turf said, meaning every word he spoke. As bad as he wanted Sosa dead right now, he had to put that issue on pause for a second and get back to the money. "In three days, we got a meeting with the connect, so I need y'all to be on standby."

Quick was trying to pay attention to what Turf was saying, but his phone kept interrupting him. Kat sent him a text message that read, Pls call me. It's an emergency!!! But he ignored it and placed his phone back into its case.

"I also got the heads-up on this stash house I'ma need you two to take care of," Turf said, looking at Major Pain and Quick.

Again, Quick's phone interrupted.

Turf looked over at Quick. "Is everything all right?"

"My bad. Let me take this call real quick," he said, and he answered his ringing phone. "Yo, what's up? Why the fuck you keep on calling me?" he barked into the phone.

"I told you I had an emergency," Kat replied with an attitude.

"What's the emergency?" Quick asked her as if she was lying.

"I can't talk right now. Just please come over to my house, please," she begged.

"A'ight, I'll be there in about a hour," Quick said, ending the call. He slipped his phone back into its case. "My bad," he apologized.

"It's all good. Just make sure you ready to put in this work in the next few days," Turf said.

Just then, Major Pain pulled up in front of a big, expensive-looking house.

"Y'all niggas hold it down," Turf said, and he and Goliath hopped out of the back of the truck and headed inside the house.

"What's good? Wanna hit up a strip club or something?" Major Pain looked over at Quick for a response.

"Nah." Quick looked at his watch. "I need you to drop me off at this chick crib," he said. "We can hit up the strip club tomorrow, if you want."

"Nah. I'm hitting that bitch up tonight," Major Pain said as he pulled off. "It's too early for me to go home."

Major Pain hated going home. He didn't have a family or a girlfriend at home waiting for him, so when he went home, it was just him. He didn't trust a woman enough to let her move into his house. He had seen some of the best hustlers lose everything because of a woman. If he was going to lose everything he had worked so hard for, it wasn't going to be because of a woman. He'd rather blow all his money before he let a woman destroy him.

"You better be careful fuckin' with them bitches," Major Pain said. "I never let a bitch know where I live."

"So you plan on living the rest of your life like that?"

"If I have to," Major Pain said seriously. "Trust me, bitches will fuck your whole shit up," he said, pulling over at the address that Quick had given him.

"You a crazy muthafucka." Quick laughed as he gave Major Pain dap and slid out of the truck. "Don't get too drunk at the strip club and take one of them strippers home with you." He laughed out loud.

"I'll never get that drunk." Major Pain pulled off once he knew Quick was at his destination.

Quick walked up the three steps slowly. He let out a frustrated breath as he knocked on the door. Seconds later, he heard feet shuffling behind the door, then the sound of locks being unlocked.

"Hey, baby. What's up?" Kat said, standing behind the door as she opened it.

Quick stepped inside the apartment and saw that all the lights were out, and Kat had candles lit up all over the place. "Fuck going on up in here?" He turned the lights on and saw Kat in a purple bra and matching thong, with purple pumps to match. And her face was covered in makeup, making her look very sexy. Quick had never seen her done up like this before.

"I missed you," Kat whined, walking up on Quick. "And I need my dick," she added in an almost begging tone as she and Quick stood face-to-face.

Immediately, Quick felt his dick begin to stiffen. "What's the big emergency?" he asked, trying to play it cool.

"This is the emergency." Kat pulled the front of her thong to the side, so Quick could see her freshly waxed pussy.

Quick looked down and pretended not to be impressed. "You called me down here for that?"

"And for this," Kat said seductively. She melted down into a squat and unzipped Quick's pants.

"Yo, chill," Quick said in weak protest.

Kat ignored Quick's words as she placed his already hard dick into her mouth and began sucking on it. She twirled her head and sucked on Quick's dick like she was in a competition to see who could make a dick come first.

As bad as Quick wanted to tell Kat to stop, his mouth just wouldn't cooperate with his brain, so he just stood there and allowed her to suck all over his dick, until he finally exploded inside her mouth.

After Quick cleaned off his dick, he headed for the door.

"Where the fuck you think you going?" Kat asked, her hands on her hips.

"I'm out. I came over here 'cause I thought you were in trouble or something."

"Fuck you mean, you out?" Kat said, her face frowned. "Nigga, you ain't going nowhere until you give me my dick." She kicked off her heels and slipped out of her bra and thong. "You must got me fucked up," she added, and she turned the lights back off.

"Yo, I'm out," Quick said as he grabbed the doorknob.

Kat quickly pushed the door closed, just as Quick was opening it. "Stop playing," she said, rubbing on Quick's muscular chest. "You can't just leave me like this. I have needs too, you know."

"Fuck that got to do with me?" Quick was tired of playing games with Kat.

"Oh, so what? You gon' go home and dream about that dead bitch you was fuckin'?" Kat said, trying to get under Quick's skin. "You must like that cold pussy." She laughed loudly. "You a bitch-ass nigga anyway," she said, looking at him in disgust. "I don't even know why I called you in the first place. You rather go beat off to a dead bitch memories than get some good pussy sitting right here in your face."

"Watch your mouth!"

"Fuck you and that dead bitch! Both of y'all can kiss my ass!" Kat yelled all up in Quick's face. "And I heard your own boy Lucky killed your bitch." She laughed loudly again. "And your bitch ass ain't even do shit. And you call yourself a man? Fuck outta here! If a bitch killed my man, I would—"

Quick smacked the shit out of Kat before she could even finish the sentence. He grabbed her by her throat and applied pressure. "Bitch, shut the fuck up! You just don't know! You just don't know!" he growled. He released his grip, shoving her backward.

Kat stumbled backward, grabbing her throat. "How dare you put your muthafuckin' hands on me!" She rushed to the phone and dialed 9-1-1.

Once Quick saw Kat pick up the phone, he made his exit.

"That's right, you bitch-ass nigga!" Kat yelled. "You better run, muthafucka! I got something for ya ass. You watch and see. You done put your hands on the wrong one!" she yelled, making a scene in her hood.

Quick ignored her threats as he flagged down a cab and headed home.

"Who That Nigga?"

Major Pain smiled as he pulled up into the strip club's parking lot. He could tell that the club was jumping just by how packed the parking lot was. After ten minutes of searching, he finally found a parking spot. He cut the engine off and checked his face through the rearview mirror. He took the 9 mm off his lap and stuck it under his seat. Then he hopped out of the truck and made his way toward the entrance.

When Major Pain reached the entrance, the big bouncer quickly stopped him. "Hold it right there!" the big man said, placing his paw on Major Pain's chest.

Major Pain looked at the bouncer like he was crazy. He brushed the big man's filthy hands off of him. "Fam, be easy."

"No, *you* be easy!" the bouncer shot back, looking down at Major Pain. "Spread your arms!" he growled, and he began patting down Major Pain for weapons.

Major Pain stood there while the big man searched him. He screwed his face up when the bouncer brushed past his testicles the second time. "Yo, fam"—Major Pain stepped back—"that's twice."

"Shut yo' bitch ass up." The bouncer stepped to the side so Major Pain could enter the club.

Major Pain stepped inside the club with a frown on his face. Before he had gotten to the club, he was in a good mood, but the bouncer at the front door had just fucked up his entire night. Major Pain's mind was already made up: when he left the club, he was going to grab his 9 mm and teach the big man a lesson.

Major Pain made his way over to the bar. He needed a drink to calm his nerves. "Yo, let me get a bottle of Rosé," he said, tossing some bills up on the counter.

The bartender placed the bottle of Rosé on the counter along with a champagne flute.

"Nah, I don't need no glass." Major Pain took the bottle off the counter. He swigged straight from the bottle as he made his way over to the wall and placed his back up against it, so he could see everything as he watched the show that the strippers put on. He bobbed his head to the sound of Lil Wayne blasting from the speakers.

Major Pain took another swig from his bottle as he watched all the action going on in the club. He watched the bouncer, who had given him trouble at the front door, roughly grab some guy up and toss him down the long flight of stairs leading to the front door. He thought the bouncer was just trying to show off in front of the strippers.

Major Pain shook his head in disgust as he watched the bouncer walk around the club trying to intimidate the customers. He made a mental note to make an example out of the big man.

Everybody in the strip club got hype when Three 6 Mafia's song, "Who Run It," came blaring through the speakers.

Major Pain bobbed his head as he sipped from his bottle. He watched a light-skin woman with a nice-looking weave make her way in his direction. She wore a pair of stilettos with a pair of fishnet stockings, and up top, her breasts hung freely. The woman and Major Pain kept eye contact with one another the whole time as she walked up to him.

Major Pain watched as the other men in the club grabbed at the light-skin woman's hand and wrist as she walked through the club.

The woman stopped directly in Major Pain's face. "What's up?" She was so close, it looked like the two were about to kiss.

Major Pain turned his head and took another swig from his bottle. "Fuck you mean, what's up?"

"I saw you watching me from all the way across the room," she said. "Were you undressing me with your eyes?"

Major Pain smiled. "Maybe," he replied. He looked closer and noticed that the woman was drop-dead gorgeous. "And if I was?"

"Then me and you might have to fight." The woman smiled, rubbing her hands on Major Pain's chest.

"Yo, what's your name, ma?" Major Pain looked at her sexy, full lips that were covered with gloss. If she wasn't a stripper, he would've kissed her in her mouth right then and there.

"Everyone calls me Apple Bottom." She turned around so Major Pain could get a good look at her fat ass.

Major Pain looked down and saw that Apple Bottom had a big butterfly tattooed on her ass.

"Oh, this my shit!" Apple Bottom slurred, throwing her hands in the air and making the wings on her butterfly flap to Fabolous's song, "You Be Killin' 'Em" blaring through the speakers.

Major Pain watched as Apple Bottom moved her body like a snake in front of him. She was looking back at him the whole time. Her eyes told him that she wanted him to fuck the shit out of her, and the way she moved her body just confirmed what her eyes were saying.

Major Pain swigged from his bottle as he watched Apple Bottom rub and grind her ass all over his package.

Lucky and Hawk sat over on the other side of the club, discussing business, getting their drink on. Since Sosa was still locked up, the two men began making decisions on their own to keep the empire afloat. But no matter what they did, they always put Sosa's cut off to the side.

"Yo, I can't believe your sister is a stripper." Lucky downed his shot in one gulp.

Hawk shrugged his shoulders. "Can't stop a muthafucka from doing what they want," he said. "She might be a stripper, but she's a good woman and has a good heart."

Lucky nodded his head, but in his mind, he told himself he had never once met a good-hearted stripper. Most of them were straight-up hustlers. Hawk's sister could've been different, but he wasn't buying it.

"Speaking of your sister," Lucky said, looking around, "where did she disappear to? I want her to hook me up with one of her stripper friends."

Hawk scanned the club for a second until he finally spotted his little sister. “She right over there,” he said, pointing in her direction.

Lucky followed Hawk’s hand and couldn’t believe who Hawk’s sister was all up on. “Yo, that’s that nigga Major Pain over there,” he said out loud.

“Major who?”

“He works with Turf,” Lucky said, knowing Major Pain was one of the men who had tried to take his life at the mansion party. He watched closely as Hawk’s sister danced with Major Pain like they were the only two in the club.

“Who, that nigga my sister dancing with?” Hawk said, his nose flared. He didn’t like how his sister was dancing with the man in the first place. He had been to the club plenty of times, and usually, his sister would just work the crowd and maybe do a little pole work, but he had never seen his sister dancing with a john the way she was dancing with this Major Pain guy.

Hawk quickly stood to his feet, and he and Lucky made their way over to the other side of the club.

Major Pain ran his free hand all over Apple Bottom’s body as he continued to grind up on her as she flowed to the beat. And he most definitely was loving the woman’s butterfly.

Apple Bottom grabbed Major Pain's hand and led him over to a sofa that could hold two. "So, what's your name?" she asked, rubbing her hand across his chest.

"Pain."

"Oh really?" Apple Bottom smiled. "As in 'hurt me' pain?"

"No. As in Major Pain." He lifted his bottle to his mouth.

"Let me see your phone real quick." Apple Bottom licked her lips.

Major Pain removed his BlackBerry from its case and handed it to the sexy woman who sat beside him. He watched as Apple Bottom stored her number inside then handed him his phone back.

"Let me finish getting this money. I'll be back over here in a few." Apple Bottom winked as she got up and walked off.

Major Pain watched as she slid onto some ugly man's lap. He smirked as he took another swig from his bottle. When he looked up again, he saw Lucky headed straight for him, along with an angry-looking man in tow.

Major Pain quickly shot to his feet and took a defensive stance. Before he knew it, Lucky had already swung on him. The two men went spilling into the rest of the crowd as they tried to take each other's heads off.

Hawk picked up a wooden stool and crashed it over Major Pain's back.

Once the fight started getting out of hand, the DJ shut off the music and called for security over the mic. "Come on, guys," he said over the mic. "Don't ruin the night."

Three big bouncers quickly ran over to the middle of the club and broke up the fight.

When the bouncer watching over the front door saw that Major Pain was the one causing trouble, he yelled, "I got him!" The big man roughly grabbed Major Pain up by the shirt and threw him into a choke hold as he escorted him over to the staircase, where he tossed him down the stairs.

The bouncer laughed as he watched Major Pain tumble down the steps and land at the bottom. "Troublemaking muthafucka!" He then trotted down the steps and picked Major Pain up again, this time, using Major Pain's head to open the front door, then tossed him out into the street like trash. "And stay out!" he barked, and he and the rest of his bouncer friends busted out laughing.

Outside, two police officers helped Major Pain to his feet. "You need an ambulance?" one of them asked.

"No, he's fine. I'll take him home," Apple Bottom said, fully dressed as she came to the rescue, and the two officers helped escort Major Pain into the backseat of Apple Bottom's Land Rover.

"Thank you so much, officers." Apple Bottom handed each officer a twenty-dollar bill and climbed behind the wheel and slowly exited the parking lot.

Quick stepped inside his apartment and saw Tiffany peacefully sleeping on the air mattress. He stared at her for a second before entering the bedroom. He was happy now that Tiffany could finally get a good night's rest. Ever since she had moved in with him, he had noticed that now she smiled more and always seemed to be happy, even when things weren't going as smoothly as she expected.

Quick stepped into the bedroom, slipped out of his clothes, and hopped into the bed. He grabbed his cell phone from the nightstand, so he could charge it. As he plugged his phone up, he saw that he had four missed calls from Kat. Quick ignored the missed calls and silently stared up at the ceiling until he finally drifted off to sleep.

The next morning, Quick awoke to the smell of some good breakfast floating throughout the house. "Damn! That shit smells good," he said, sliding out of the bed. He made his way to the living room.

"Hey, sorry," Tiffany apologized. "I hope I didn't wake you up."

"Don't mention it." Quick waved her off. "I didn't know you could cook like this," he said, looking at the pancakes, turkey bacon, and scrambled eggs.

"It's a lot of things you don't know about me." Tiffany smirked as she made her plate along with Quick's.

The two took a seat on the floor and enjoyed their breakfast.

"Damn!" Quick moaned as he destroyed his meal like an animal. He couldn't remember the last time he'd had a home-cooked meal.

Tiffany laughed. "Slow down." She had never had someone appreciate her cooking like this before. She used to cook for Blake, but most of the time, he would never eat.

"This the best breakfast I done had in a while. I might can get used to this."

"Oh really?" Tiffany smiled at Quick as he sipped his orange juice. "Can I ask you a question?"

"Shoot."

"How come you never tried to come on to me?"

The question kind of caught Quick off guard. "I mean," he began, stalling for time, "I'm not really looking for all that right now. Right before you moved in"—he paused, shaking his head—"my girlfriend, who I had been with for a while, had just been murdered not too long ago."

"I'm sorry. I didn't know."

"It's okay," Quick said, flashing a friendly smile. "You didn't know."

"Well, I just want to say thanks for not pushing up on me and making me feel welcome. I really appreciate it," she said sincerely.

"It's nothing," Quick said as he finished his breakfast. He knew that both of them were just getting over past situations. That's why he didn't mind letting her share the apartment with him.

"I would like to take you out tonight," Tiffany said as she stood to her feet. She took Quick's empty plate and set it in the sink.

"Take me out tonight?" Quick repeated with a smile.

"Yes, take you out tonight," Tiffany said, returning to her seat on the floor. "I was thinking dinner and a movie, to show my appreciation for everything you have done for me."

"You sure you wanna do that? I ain't no cheap date."

Tiffany returned his smile. "It's the least I can do."

"Okay, then it's a date," Quick said as he stood to his feet. "I gotta make a few runs, but I'll definitely be back for our date," he added before disappearing inside the bathroom.

Kat pulled up in front of her old projects and let the engine die. She was still pissed about Quick putting his hands on her, but she was even more upset that he wouldn't take any of her calls. How dare he treat her like this after all the two of them had been through?

She hopped out of her car. "I got something for his ass," she said to herself as she made her way inside the building. She reached the lobby and repeatedly pressed the call button for the elevator.

Kat stepped off the elevator with a frown on her face. She made her way down the hallway and stopped in front of the door she was looking for. She knocked on the door and patiently waited for an answer.

Seconds later, a tall, dark-skin man wearing no shirt answered the door. He was a well-built man, with a head full of waves. On the side of his face was a scar from a cut he'd received while serving time in an upstate correctional facility.

"What the fuck you want?" the man said dryly.

"Oh, so I can't even come and visit my own cousin now?" Kat said, brushing past the muscular man.

"I'm only your cousin when you need something. So what's up?" Tommy asked.

In the streets, they called him Tommy Gunz. He was feared and respected, because he was known for his gun going off. Tommy Gunz lived for action and was always caught up in some kind of drama.

"I got a little problem," Kat said as she walked over to the couch and helped herself to a seat. As she sat down, she noticed Tommy had a shotgun as well as three other guns lying on top of his coffee table. "Do you really need all of these guns?"

"They don't call me Tommy Gunz for nothing." He smirked as he took a seat on the opposite couch. "Now what's on your mind?"

"It's Quick," Kat started. "This nigga done lost his mind and put his hands on me 'cause I didn't want to give him no pussy," she lied.

Tommy Gunz lit up a Newport. "Damn! You still with that cat?"

"No. Fuck him!" Kat was still madly in love with Quick, but she still hated him at the same time.

"Okay, so I'm going to ask you again. What is it that you want me to do?"

"Depends," Kat said with a wicked smile. "You trying to make some money?"

"I'm listening," Tommy said, sitting up in his seat.

"Well, I heard that now Quick is working for Turf. So I know he's got to be holding. I say we just find out where he's living, find out who he's sleeping with, and take it from there."

"So, basically, you want me to rob your ex-boyfriend and hope he's got a stash?"

"Trust me, I know Quick. And he's definitely got a stash. The only problem is, we going to have to find it. I know you not scared," she said, fucking with his ego.

"Scared?" Tommy looked over at Kat like she was crazy. "Tommy Gunz ain't scared of nobody or nothing, in case you ain't know so. But you know, if it's bread involved, then you can count me in."

"Great," Kat said as she stood to her feet. "See what you can find out, and I'll do the same. Then at the end of the week, we'll see what's up."

"Deal," Tommy Gunz said, and the two shook hands.

***

Quick entered the trap house and saw Spike sitting on a milk crate, leaning back against the wall. Spike spoke, but Quick just replied with a quick head nod. He wasn't really in a talking mood. His job was to make sure things ran smoothly and that the money was always correct.

"How that bread looking?" Quick asked.

"The count is straight," Spike replied, tossing him a thick stack of money.

Quick caught the stack and quickly thumbed through it. He stuffed the money into a small book bag that he carried. At the same time, he heard a loud knock at the door. "Go see who that is," he said as he heard another hard knock on the door.

When Spike finally reached the back door, he snatched it open with an attitude. "Bitch, why the fuck is you banging on the muthafuckin' door like you crazy?" he barked. He grabbed the frail woman by her shirt and snatched her inside the trap house.

"Bitch, get your hands off me!" the fiend snapped. "It's bad enough y'all got me walking all the way around to the back door. The least y'all could do is answer the muthafucka," she said in a slur.

Quick stepped in. "How can we help you?"

"You can help me by giving me four of the biggest bags y'all got up in this muthafucka," the fiend said, talking louder than she needed to. She counted out thirty-eight dollars.

Quick smiled. "What's your name?" he asked as Spike went to the back to get the product.

"Why? You taking me out on a date?" the fiend said, flashing a rotten-tooth smile. "You are kind of handsome." She reached for Quick's face.

Quick quickly caught her hands in midair. "If I met you fifteen, twenty years ago, I might've considered it," he lied, making the filthy-looking woman feel good about herself.

Spike came and handed the woman her product and took her money. "Nah, hold up, bitch!" he barked, stopping the fiend at the door. "You short."

"She good for it," Quick said, winking at the fiend.

Spike sucked his teeth, upset that the fiend escaped without an ass whipping. He couldn't stand the loud-talking fiend and was looking for any reason to put his hands on the woman.

"Man, listen," Spike began. "I run a tight ship around here. I can't be having fiends coming up short, thinking it's cool."

Quick ignored Spike's comment as he began scrolling through his BlackBerry. His mind was on Tiffany and their dinner and movie date. He glanced down at his watch and decided that it was time for him to leave.

"Hold it down, young'un," he said, and he exited the trap house and headed home.

***

Major Pain woke up the next day, not knowing where he was. He quickly reached for his waistband to grab his gun but stopped when he realized he was naked.

"Where the fuck am I?" he said to himself as he mustered up enough strength to get out of the bed.

Major Pain walked through the house butt naked, hoping to find the owner of the house. As he made his way downstairs, he could hear the sounds of the singer Monica humming softly through the speakers. He walked through the spacious living room, until he reached the kitchen, where he saw Apple Bottom standing over the stove as she sipped from her wineglass.

"Yo," he said, causing her to jump at the sound of his voice.

"Hey." Apple Bottom looked down at Major Pain's package. "You hungry?"

"Where are my clothes?" Major Pain said in an even tone. He looked around the house and saw that Apple Bottom was doing pretty well for herself.

"They had blood on them, so I washed them for you. They're in the dryer," Apple Bottom, said, leading the way to her laundry room.

Major Pain followed her throughout the house butt naked. Apple Bottom wore a wifebeater and a pair of pink boy shorts. Her hair was pulled back in a neat ponytail, and she walked barefoot on the soft, thick carpet.

Apple Bottom removed Major Pain's clothes from the dryer and plugged in the iron. On top of her washing machine was everything that was inside Major Pain's pockets.

"Your money, car keys, and everything else you had in your pockets is right there on top of the washing machine," she said, nodding toward his things.

"I got it." Major Pain put his drawers back on, grabbed the iron, and began to iron his jeans.

"You all right?" Apple Bottom asked.

"I'm good." Major Pain was embarrassed by the fact that the beautiful woman had seen him get his ass whipped. He'd recognized Lucky, but he didn't know who the other man was. It didn't matter though. The mystery man and Lucky were both living on borrowed time.

"I'm going to have a word with Benny later on tonight. What he did to you wasn't right, and I'ma let him know about himself." Apple Bottom sipped on her wine.

"Who the fuck is Benny?" Major Pain asked, slipping into his jeans.

"The ugly-ass bouncer that tossed you down the stairs." Apple Bottom shook her head. "He's always in a bad mood 'cause none of the girls who work at the club will give his ass play."

Major Pain smirked. "Don't worry about that clown." He slipped on his wifebeater. He had big plans for Mr. Benny. Just thinking about what he was going to do to the big man brought a wicked smile to his face. "Thanks for everything," Major Pain said as he hugged Apple Bottom.

"I fried all that chicken. You better come and help me eat this shit," she said, looking at him like he was crazy. She led the way back to the kitchen, where she poured two glasses of wine and set them on the table. Then she started to make their plates.

Major Pain looked down at the fried chicken and baked mac and cheese. "Damn! I didn't know strippers knew how to cook."

"And what's that supposed to mean?" Apple Bottom asked as she bit down on her chicken. "Just because I dance for a living means I can't or don't know how to cook?"

"I didn't say that," Major Pain said, quickly stopping her in her tracks. "It's just that usually, most strippers I meet don't cook. They're more into the takeout thing."

"Well, yes, I know how to cook." Apple Bottom playfully rolled her eyes. "My mother made sure she taught me how to cook."

"I see," Major Pain said as he punished the food that sat in front of him. If it was one thing he loved, it was a woman who knew how to cook. "So, Apple Bottom, what's your real name?"

Apple Bottom smiled. “My name is Nicole, but you can call me Nikki.”

Major Pain smiled as he pushed away from the table. “Thanks for the food, Nikki. It was delicious, but I must be going,” he said as he headed for the door.

“That’s it?” Nikki asked as she followed Major Pain to the door.

Major Pain turned to face her. He noticed that even without her makeup on, she was still beautiful. “That’s it, what?”

“So what? You just going to leave like that?” she asked with her hands on her hips.

“Oh, my bad.” Major Pain reached down into his pocket and peeled off a few bills and held them out to her.

But Nikki smacked the money out of his hand and watched the bills float to the floor. “I don’t want, nor do I need, your money,” she said in a matter-of-fact tone. “You know what? Just get out.” She held the door open.

Major Pain looked down at the bills then turned and left Nikki standing there. Once he was out the door, she slammed it and stormed to her room, where she lay across the bed feeling stupid. “I should’ve left his ass for dead,” she said to herself as she closed her eyes and relaxed before it was time for her to go to work.

"A Little Unfinished Business"

Quick stepped foot into his apartment and stood in shock as he saw Tiffany dressed up for the first time. She wore a tight red skirt that dropped to around the middle of her thighs, and on her feet, she wore a pair of knee-high red boots with a three-inch heel.

"You like?" she asked, spinning around in place.

"You look great."

With what Tiffany was wearing, Quick got a chance to see what she was really working with. To say he was impressed would've been an understatement. He disappeared in the back, where he took a quick shower and got dressed.

Thirty minutes later, the two headed out the door. Quick opened the passenger door and watched Tiffany melt into the seat. Then he hopped into the driver's seat and turned the car on. Joe Budden's mixtape, *Mood Muzik 4*, flowed through the speakers as he pulled out onto the street.

"So what you wanna do first, dinner or go to the movies?"

"Umm . . . " Tiffany thought on it. "I guess we can go to the movies first."

"Let's do it." Quick smiled as he hopped onto the highway. "Can you do me a favor?"

"Yeah. Wassup?"

"Reach in the back and get those cups and pour me a drink."

Tiffany leaned back in the back, grabbed the half-empty bottle of Cîroc and the pack of foam cups, and poured Quick a drink.

"Good looking," he said, accepting the drink. He sipped lightly as he kept his eyes on the road.

As Quick drove, he checked Tiffany out on the low. He loved how she always seemed to be in a positive mood, no matter what was going on. She was beautiful inside and out.

Tiffany poured herself a cup, and she set the bottle back on the backseat.

"Damn! This shit is strong," she said after taking a sip. She was holding her chest because it was burning her so much.

Tiffany bobbed her head to the music as she continued to get her sip on. She found herself starting to like Quick. She'd tried to talk herself out of it, but the feelings were too strong. She had been with Blake for so long, she'd forgotten how a real man was supposed to treat a woman. And Quick treated her like a queen, even though she wasn't his queen, and that's what she appreciated the most about him.

"Damn! This muthafucka is packed," Quick said as he cruised through the parking lot, searching for a parking spot.

After about ten minutes of searching, he finally found a spot. He and Tiffany finished up their drinks then hopped out and headed toward the entrance so they could get their tickets.

When they reached the window, Quick dug down into his pocket to pay for the tickets, but Tiffany quickly stopped him.

"Nah, I got this," she said, removing a twenty and ten-dollar bill from her purse and handing it to the woman that stood behind the glass. The woman gladly took Tiffany's money and handed her back her change, along with two tickets.

Quick and Tiffany stepped inside and made their way straight to the concession stand, where they ordered some chicken fingers, cheese fries, and two slushies.

"This movie better be good too," Quick said as they entered the theater.

They rounded the corner and saw that the theater was packed. Tiffany sucked her teeth. She hated when the movie theater was packed like this.

After climbing up a few steps, they found three empty seats on the end. They took their seats, leaving one seat next to Quick open.

Quick leaned over and grabbed a piece of chicken. He stood up when the previews came on. "Be right back," he said. "I gotta pee."

"A'ight, hurry up." Tiffany watched Quick bop down the steps and bend the corner. "He better hurry up if he want any of these cheese fries," she said to herself as she dug into the fries.

After she finished stuffing her face, she grabbed a napkin and cleaned her hands. When she looked up, she saw a man and a woman stop at her row.

The man asked, "Yo, somebody sitting here?"

Before Tiffany could even answer, the man and his girl sat down in Quick's seat and the empty seat.

"Excuse me!" Tiffany said, looking at the couple like they had lost their minds. "My man was sitting right there." The word *man* had slipped from her lips.

"Well, I guess now ya man going to have to find another seat," the man said. "You move your feet, you lose your seat," he said, and he and his girlfriend busted out laughing.

Before Tiffany got a chance to reply, she saw Quick making his way back up the steps with a confused look on his face.

"Fuck going on over here?" Quick asked, standing over the couple.

"Go find you a seat and sit down," the man said.

"You sitting in my seat," Quick said, looking down at the man.

"Fam, if you don't mind, me and my lady trying to watch the movie," the man said, as if Quick was becoming an annoyance.

The man's girlfriend sucked her teeth. "Damn! Why you standing over me like that?"

With the speed of an alley cat, Quick turned and smacked the shit out of the girl for talking to him sideways, causing her man to jump up out of his seat. Quick caught the man with a swift two-piece before the man grabbed him, and the two went tumbling down the stairs.

As the other girl looked on in shock as her man and Quick went tumbling down the stairs, Tiffany sucker punched her from behind. She grabbed a handful of the woman's weave with one hand, while she went to work on her with her free hand, talking shit the whole time.

After five minutes of brawling, movie theater security finally came and broke the two couples up.

"You all right?" Quick asked, once he and Tiffany stepped outside.

"Yeah, I'm good," Tiffany replied with a smile. "Thanks for holding me down back there."

Quick opened the passenger door so Tiffany could step inside.

"You know I'm going to hold you down."

Quick smiled as he pulled off. It felt good to have a rider in his corner, someone who would have his back no matter what was going on.

"I didn't know you could fight like that." Quick looked over at Tiffany. "I thought you was going to kill that girl for a second," he joked.

"Nah. I ain't like how they just tried to come debo your seat like that." She laughed, but the truth was, she had a whole bunch of built-up rage inside of her from when Blake used to beat her ass, so when the couple had pulled that stunt, she took out all of her frustration on the woman.

Quick and Tiffany's laugh was interrupted when Quick heard his cell phone ringing.

"Yo. What up?" he answered.

"Where you at?" Major Pain asked on the other line.

"On the road right now. Why? What's up?" Quick asked. Just by the sound of Major Pain's voice, Quick knew something was wrong.

"I need your help. Meet me over at the spot in a hour," Major Pain said, ending the call.

Quick placed his phone back inside his case, and immediately, Tiffany could see something was wrong. "Everything all right?" she asked.

"Nah. I'm going to have to cancel dinner tonight. Something came up. Sorry."

"It's okay. I understand. Business comes first," Tiffany told him.

Quick pulled up in front of their apartment and placed the car in park. "Thanks for taking me out tonight. I had a wonderful time. Sorry we had to cut it short though."

"You are more than welcome." Tiffany smiled. "But you owe me dinner," she said as she slid out of the car.

"Deal."

Quick waited until Tiffany was inside the apartment before he pulled off. He didn't know what Major Pain wanted, but from the sound of his voice, he could tell it was important.

Quick bobbed his head to music as he cruised down the highway. It didn't take long for his mind to start wondering to Tiffany. He'd had a wonderful time with the woman tonight, even though the night ended with them having a brawl. He was just starting to realize how much of a good woman she really was. Not to mention, he loved how she had his back during the brawl. He tried his hardest to shake Tiffany from his mind, but that task was easier said than done.

He pulled up in front of the spot and saw Major Pain sitting on the hood of his car, dressed in all black. In his hand was a blunt, and on his face was the look of murder.

He hopped out of his car and gave Major Pain dap. "What's good, my nigga?"

"I need you to come take a ride with me," Major Pain said as he got behind the wheel of his car. Once Quick was in the passenger seat, he pulled off.

"What happened to your face?" Quick asked, noticing that Major Pain had something heavy on his mind.

"I bumped into your boy Lucky last night." Major Pain smirked.

"What happened?"

"We ran into each other in the strip club," Major Pain said, slowing down for the red light. "I saw him, and I popped off. Then out the blue, his man came out of nowhere and snuffed me." He pulled into the parking lot of the strip club.

"So what we getting into tonight?" Quick asked, confused as the two sat in the strip club's parking lot.

"You see that big, ugly fuck right there?" Major Pain pointed at the bouncer standing by the entrance. "Me and him got a little unfinished business," he said, replaying the scene from the other night over and over again in his mind. Benny had violated him, and now he had to pay for his actions.

At the end of the night, Benny walked through the parking lot to his run-down van. He hopped behind the wheel and cruised slowly through the parking lot, following one of the new strippers, who was walking over to the corner to flag down a cab.

"Hey, beautiful," he called out. "You need a ride?"

"Nah, I'm good," the stripper said politely, not bothering to stop.

Benny pressed. "You sure? I mean, it won't be no trouble. It's late, and you are looking kind of sexy. I wouldn't want anybody to try and snatch you up. No way I'd be able to forgive myself."

"I said I'm good." The stripper stuck her arm out, trying to flag down a cab.

Benny sucked his teeth as he recklessly stormed out of the parking lot. "Stuck-up-ass bitches!"

Benny had been working at the strip club for eight months now and still hadn't been able to get one stripper to give him some play. He was tired of masturbating and paying for pussy. He needed some in-house pussy. He pulled up in front of his building, where he lived in a one-bedroom apartment.

He stepped out of his van and slipped a cigarette between his lips before putting fire to the end of it. He turned and hog-spat on the ground before entering his building.

"Yo, fam, hold that door!" he heard someone yell.

Benny looked and saw a young man jogging toward the building. He held the door as the man entered the building.

"Good looking," Quick said, catching his breath.

"No problem," Benny said, and he and the young man walked toward the elevator, where Benny pressed the call button.

"Excuse me, but if you don't mind, can you put that cigarette out?" Quick asked politely.

"Fuck off!" Benny said, waving the young man off. "If you don't like the smoke, then I suggest you take the fuckin' stairs, cocksucker." He sized the man up. He knew if the man was feeling froggy, he wouldn't have any wins against him, not even on a bad day.

"Damn! It's not that serious," Quick said with a smirk on his face.

Benny was tired of hearing the man's mouth. "You say another word, and I'm going to give you a serious ass whipping."

When the elevator came, the two men stepped inside and stood on opposite sides. Benny pressed for the fifth floor, and Quick pressed for the sixth floor.

The elevator came to a stop on the fifth floor, and Benny stepped off. Before he was fully out of the elevator, he felt the cold barrel of a gun pressed to the back of his head.

He quickly threw his hands up in surrender. "Chill out, youngblood. I was just fuckin' with you back there," he said, fear dripping from his voice.

"Shut the fuck up!" Quick barked as he dug into the big man's pocket and removed his keys. "Which one of these raggedy muthafuckas is yours?"

Benny nodded, and Quick shoved him in the direction he had nodded.

He handed Benny the keys. "Open it!"

Once inside the apartment, Quick made the big man lie face down on the floor. Then he pulled out his phone and made a quick phone call.

"Youngblood, what's this all about?" Benny asked nervously.

A strong kick to the face hushed the big man.

Minutes later, Benny heard another man enter the apartment. He looked up and almost shit on himself.

"You don't look too happy to see me." Major Pain smiled. He removed his hoodie from his head, squatted in front of the big man, and shook his head. "I would hate to be you right now."

"Come on, man. You know I didn't mean nothing by that shit the other night," Benny said, pleading for his life. "I was just doing my job."

"Of course, you didn't." Major Pain flashed a wicked smile as he stood up and screwed a silencer onto the barrel of his 9 mm.

"Please don't do this," Benny begged, tears streaming down his face.

"Stop all that crying!" Major Pain barked as he sent a bullet into the back of Benny's thigh. "You wasn't crying when you tossed me down the stairs, was you?" Major Pain turned the big man over onto his back.

Benny was about to say something, but a blow to the head made him lose his train of thought.

Quick leaned back on the wall and just shook his head as he watched Major Pain stomp the big man repeatedly. He didn't know what the big man had done, but by the way Major Pain was whipping his ass, he must've done something. After stomping the shit out of the big man for almost ten minutes, Major Pain emptied his whole clip into Benny's face.

"You done?" Quick asked, looking down at Benny's lifeless body. He had never seen a man get beat the way Major Pain had beat the big man.

"That muthafucka lucky I got tired."

Major Pain was breathing heavily as the two men exited the apartment. Killing Benny had made him feel good inside. Taking a life had never felt so good. Next on his list was Lucky.

"What you getting yourself into tonight?"

"Shit," Quick said. "I'm just gon' go home and chill."

"Fuck. I'ma probably do the same," Major Pain said as he dropped Quick off at his car.

Quick stepped into the crib and saw Tiffany with a towel wrapped around her upper body as she applied lotion to her legs.

"Damn!" he said to himself as he took in her beauty. "My bad. I didn't mean to bust in on you like that."

"It's okay," Tiffany said. "It's your house."

When she saw Quick heading to the back room, she stopped him. "Um, do you mind rubbing some lotion on my back for me?"

"I think I can handle that."

Quick removed his jacket and hung it up before heading over and taking a seat on the air mattress. He watched as Tiffany lay face down on the air mattress, her towel covering her ass, while up top, she was completely nude. He squeezed some lotion into his hands and began rubbing it on her back.

"So how was your day?" Tiffany asked, her eyes closed. Quick had magic fingers. It had been so long since the last time she had gotten a massage.

"It was okay," he told her. "Just had to take care of a li'l something-something."

"Well, I'm just glad you are okay." Tiffany just loved the way he cared for her and treated her with nothing but respect, even though they weren't sleeping with one another.

"Why wouldn't I be okay?"

"Well, I know what you do, and sometimes, I find myself worrying about you."

"You have nothing to worry about." Quick chuckled. "I'm going to be fine. Thanks for caring though," he said as he applied more lotion to his hand. Tiffany's skin was soft like a baby's.

Quick had eyes for Tiffany, but he hadn't let her move in just so he could sleep with her. He just genuinely wanted to help her, and that's why he hadn't pushed up on her.

"I think I'm starting to like you more than I should," Tiffany admitted.

She couldn't help how she felt about him and was tired of fighting it. She flipped over on her back so she could look at Quick, and she saw his eyes glance down at her breasts then back up to her eyes.

"I want to be your woman. I want to take care of you, and I want to be all that you need," she told him. "You are the only man that has ever treated me like a woman and made me feel good about myself, like I'm worth something, and I would like to repay you by you letting me be your girl and allowing me to show you what I have to offer."

Quick was at a loss for words. He couldn't believe what he was hearing. Tiffany was a beautiful woman, who he knew, given the opportunity, would treat him like nothing other than a king.

"You sure you ready to jump into another relationship, especially after the one you just got out of?" he asked, looking into her eyes. He knew Blake had put her through hell and back and just wanted to make sure she was sure she was ready for this.

Tiffany sat up on the air mattress. “Blake ain’t half the man you are, and I just want to love someone who’s going to appreciate everything I have to offer and all I do.”

She leaned in and kissed Quick’s lips. He tried to pull away, but she pulled him into her and kissed him again. This time, Quick kissed her back as his hands made their way to her breasts.

Tiffany let out a light moan as Quick’s lips found their way to her neck. Immediately, she could feel her pussy get moist as the two continued to kiss passionately.

Quick made his way from Tiffany’s lips, down to her neck, to her breasts, to her belly button, then from her belly button down to her freshly waxed pussy that sat up looking at him. He spread her legs apart as he buried his face in her pussy.

“Oh my God!” Tiffany moaned as she grabbed the back of Quick’s head as he licked and sucked all over her clitoris. She raised her hips, so Quick’s face could be at a better angle while he pleased her.

After sucking and licking all over Tiffany’s pussy for twenty minutes, Quick climbed on top of her. Tiffany groaned when she felt him enter her walls. She gripped his back like she would fall to her death if she let go. Quick hadn’t been inside of her for seven full minutes, and she had already come.

Tiffany wrapped her thick legs around Quick as he slid in and out of her nice and slow. He made sure, with each stroke, he made her feel his entire nine inches. Once he had her worked in, he raised her legs back to her shoulders and began to pound her insides. The louder Tiffany moaned, the harder he pounded away, until he couldn't take it any more.

Quick pulled out and was getting ready to come on Tiffany's stomach, but she quickly sat up and placed her mouth on his dick just as he was coming.

"Mmmmmm!" Quick moaned as Tiffany sucked all the come out of his dick. When she was done, he playfully rolled off the bed, breathing heavily. "Damn!"

Tiffany ran to the garbage and spat. She came back, smiling from ear to ear. "That was the best," she said. She went and got herself something to drink from the kitchen before returning to Quick's side, where she curled up into his arms. That night was the first night in a very long time that she went to sleep with a smile on her face.

"Change of Plans"

Lucky parked his new Camaro in front of the projects. He tucked his .40-cal. into his waistband as he and Hawk exited the vehicle. The two men strolled through the projects and saw fiends running around all over the place.

"Damn! We might have to set up shop in this muthafucka," Hawk said out loud.

Little did Hawk know, Lucky was thinking the exact same thing.

Hawk looked over toward the next building and saw what looked like some wannabes serving the fiends right out in the open.

Lucky and Hawk ignored the men as they disappeared into the building they were looking for. The two men took the steps until they reached the floor they were looking for.

When they reached the apartment they were looking for, Lucky looked both ways before knocking on the door.

Twenty seconds later, the door swung open, and Kat stood on the other side. “Glad you could make it on such short notice,” she said, stepping to the side so the two men could enter.

“What you call me down here for?” Lucky asked once he stepped into the living room. He saw a man sitting over on the couch with a pair of leather gloves on his hands. “And who the fuck is he?” he asked, looking over at the man sitting on the couch.

“Oh, that’s just my cousin, Tommy,” Kat told him as everyone sat down.

“I ain’t got all day,” Lucky said. “So what’s up?” Just from the look on Kat’s face, he could tell she had some grimy shit up her sleeve and was more than likely ready to double-cross somebody.

“You wanna make some money?” Kat asked him, knowing she couldn’t just come straight out and tell him what she wanted to.

“What did you have in mind?” Lucky asked, keeping a close eye on Tommy. Something about the man wearing the black gloves didn’t sit right with him.

“I want to rob Quick,” Kat began. “But I need your help finding him.”

Lucky chuckled. “You called me down here ’cause you want to rob Quick, and you want me to help you?”

"All I need you to do is tell me where I can find him at," Kat said.

"And why the fuck would I do that?"

"Because whatever we get from that cocksucker, we going to kick out forty percent to you," Tommy Gunz said, speaking for the first time. "All I need you to do is lead me in the right direction."

"That muthafucka put his hands on me, and now he got to pay," Kat added.

Lucky didn't want to sic the wolves on Quick, because the two used to be the best of friends, but since he was with Hawk, it wouldn't look right if he protected him right now. That was still his friend, but they played for different teams in this game with no rules.

"The reason I came to you was because I heard you shot his bitch, so I figured, why not split the money with you," Kat said. "I'm pretty sure if you two ain't speaking no more, it's because he probably fucked you over like he did me."

"When the last time you spoke to that clown?" Hawk asked.

"I haven't spoke to that nigga in about seven to eight months," Lucky said, thinking back. But he knew the real reason why Quick refused to take his calls. Lucky had killed his woman. Of course, it had been by mistake, but by the way Quick was acting and shutting him out, he apparently didn't think it was a mistake. He must've thought that Lucky was sent there to kill her in retaliation for the shooting that went down at the mansion.

"Plus," Kat added, "I heard Quick fuckin' with Turf now, so I know he's holding."

"So, you in or what?" Tommy Gunz asked, his patience running thin.

Lucky thought on it for a second before he replied, "I'm in, and I want my cut."

"You know I got you, Lucky," Kat said, a huge smile on her face.

"I don't know where he rest his head, but what I do know is, he messing with a waitress that works in IHOP named Tiffany," Lucky said, and he and Hawk stood to their feet and headed for the door.

Tommy Gunz stopped the two men before they could leave. "Thanks. I appreciate that," he said, and he shook the two men's hands.

"Thanks, my ass," Lucky said, looking Tommy Gunz up and down. "Just make sure you have my forty percent," he said as he and Hawk made their exit.

Once the two men left, Kat and Tommy Gunz gave each other a high five. Lucky had given them the information they needed to come up. Now all they had to do was come up with a good plan and execute it.

Lucky and Hawk stepped out of the building and faced the cold chill that awaited them. As Lucky walked, he thought about Quick. He felt bad about the info he had just given up. He could tell that the man who called himself Tommy Gunz took what he did seriously, and the hungry look in his eyes told Lucky that he really needed the money.

As Lucky and Hawk exited the building, they saw a couple walking down the walkway, coming toward the building.

When Lucky passed the couple, he craned his neck to get a good look at the woman's ass. "Damn!" he said loudly. "She holding!"

Immediately, the woman's man stopped dead in his tracks. "What?" he said, removing his coat.

The woman tried to hold her man back, but it was too late. Lucky had already swung on the man.

The blow caught the man on his temple, causing him to stumble. Before he could catch his balance, Hawk finished him off with a wild haymaker. The man's head hit the concrete and bounced twice like a basketball.

The man's girlfriend screamed as she started swinging wildly on Hawk, who swiftly ducked, scooped her legs from under her, and dumped her on her head.

***

Ralph stepped out of the building and saw a few of his workers posted up in front of the building, getting it in. Ever since he had put the new product in the hood, his profit had skyrocketed. Ralph went through hell to take over the projects, and now all his hard work was finally paying off.

"How it's looking out here?" he asked, giving his young soldiers dap.

"Shit been jumping like the playoffs," Jay said. Jay was Ralph's best worker/soldier and mentally ahead of all the other workers.

"That's what I like to hear."

Just then, Ralph heard a woman's scream. He looked over toward the next building and saw two men beating up on a nice-looking couple. "Who the fuck is these clowns over there making the hood hot?" he asked, looking at his crew.

"Nah, I don't know them niggas," Jay announced.

"Fuck wrong with these niggas?" Ralph huffed as he and his crew headed over toward the next building.

Lucky searched the unconscious man's pockets, removing anything of value. Once he had all the man's goods, he walked over and snatched Hawk off the woman. Hawk had attacked the woman like she was a man.

"That's enough!" Lucky barked.

Hawk looked up and saw a group of men making their way over to them, angry looks on their faces.

"What the fuck going on over here?" Ralph looked down to the couple then back to the two men.

"None of your fuckin' business." Hawk spat on the ground right in front of Ralph.

"This my hood right here," Ralph said, pointing at the ground. "Everything that goes on in here is my business. Now I'm going to ask you niggas nicely"—he paused—"get the fuck up outta here!"

Hawk sighed loudly and hog-spat in Ralph's face. "Fuck you and your hood!"

Ralph wiped his face and swiftly removed a rusty-looking .357 from his waist and pointed it at Hawk, who reached for his waist, but two shots to his chest had already put him down before he got a chance to draw his weapon.

Lucky ducked and got low as he ran back toward his Camaro. He sent four reckless shots over his shoulder as he quickly hid behind a parked car. Two of his four shots had hit and killed two of Ralph's men.

Ralph and his crew quickly scrambled away from the scene after the gunshots finished ringing out.

Lucky looked over and saw Hawk laid out on the concrete. "Fuck!" he cursed as he hopped into the Camaro and peeled off.

Tiffany stood in the shower and let the warm water run all over her body. For the first time in her life, she was finally happy. She had a real man in her life, not somebody with ulterior motives. Not only that, but she and Quick got along really well together, and she found herself falling more and more in love with him every day.

She dried off and stepped out of the bathroom butt naked. She walked into the room and saw Quick sitting on the bed playing *Madden*.

"You still playing that game?" Tiffany smiled as she shook her head and began to lotion her body.

"Muthafuckas is cheating," Quick said as he saved his season and cut the game off.

He watched as Tiffany finished lotioning up her body. Once she was done, she threw on a pair of boy shorts and walked over to the closet. She pulled out her work uniform and laid it across the bed.

She looked up and saw Quick staring at her. "Why you looking at me like that?"

"We need a bigger place." Quick looked around at how packed the small closet was.

"I'm okay, baby." Tiffany walked over and hugged and kissed Quick. "I don't mind staying here as long as I'm with you. I'm fine."

"I know, baby. I just think it's time for a change," Quick told her. He didn't want his girl cramped up in a one-bedroom apartment. And little did Tiffany know, he didn't want her working at IHOP anymore. No girlfriend of his had to work in a fast-food restaurant; that's the reason he worked so hard, so the people he loved didn't have to.

"When is your next day off?"

"Tomorrow," Tiffany replied as she put her uniform on.

"A'ight, bet. Tomorrow, I need you to go out and find a house that you like." Quick kissed Tiffany on the lips, grabbed his jacket, and headed out the door.

Tiffany smiled in the mirror as she finished up her hair. She had never had anybody care for her as much as Quick did. If it weren't for him, she didn't know where she would be right about now. All she knew was, she was thankful to have a good man like Quick in her life, especially when she needed him most.

Tommy Gunz and Kat sat in the IHOP parking lot, waiting for Quick's new girlfriend to arrive.

The two of them had been sitting there patiently for the past two hours. The one thing Tommy Gunz couldn't figure out was, if Quick was making so much money, why was his girl waiting tables at IHOP?

"You sure that nigga Lucky was telling us the truth about Quick's new girl?"

"Yeah. Lucky don't play when it comes to his money," Kat told him. "Besides, him and Quick been fell out long before me and you came up with this plan."

"But why the fuck would he have his girl working at IHOP?" Tommy Gunz asked.

Kat sighed loudly as she pulled out her cell phone and Googled the number for the IHOP they were sitting in front of.

"We about to find out right now," Kat said as she dialed the number and waited for an answer. "Yes, hello. Can I speak to Tiffany, please?" she asked politely.

"She didn't get here yet, but she should be here within the next ten, fifteen minutes," the woman on the other line said.

"Thank you so much," Kat said, ending the call. "Yeah, we at the right spot," she said to Tommy Gunz with a smile. "She should be coming through here any minute now."

Tommy Gunz lit up another cigarette as he continued to click the hammer on his .357 back and forth. He made a mental note to inflict as much pain on Tiffany as possible for making him wait. His pockets were feeling light right now, and he was getting desperate.

Two minutes later, a chick with a short haircut and a healthy ass strolled through the parking lot.

"I think this is our girl right here," Tommy Gunz said, motioning his head in the woman's direction.

Kat looked at the woman and smiled. "Yeah, that's her."

"How you know?"

Kat applied some lip gloss to her already shiny lips. "Because I know what kind of women he likes, and that's definitely her." Immediately, she visualized Quick having sex with Tiffany the way he used to have sex with her, and just the thought of that made her angry.

"Shorty is looking a'ight," Tommy Gunz said as he watched Tiffany strut inside the restaurant.

Kat sucked her teeth. "I've seen better," she said, not liking Quick's new girlfriend one bit.

Kat and Tommy Gunz waited for another thirty minutes before they entered the restaurant, where they were escorted to a booth over in the corner. The two kept a close eye on Tiffany, Tommy Gunz's mind on the money, Kat's on inflicting pain on Quick's new girlfriend.

"We got this muthafucka now," Tommy Gunz said out loud. "Now all we have to do is let her lead us to the money."

Quick stood in a dark alley, leaning up against his car as he watched Major Pain beat the blood out of a Spanish cat that owed Turf a few thousand dollars. He never understood why someone would play with a person's money who they know would kill them if they didn't pay up. He continued to look on as Major Pain went to work on the man.

"You better tell me something," Major Pain huffed, breathing heavily.

Just as the man went to reply, Major Pain quickly kicked him in the face. "Don't waste my time. If you open up your mouth, something good better come out of it."

"All I need is another week," the man pleaded with his hands together as if he were praying.

"Another week?" Major Pain punched the man in his face repeatedly, until Quick came over and stopped him.

Quick searched the man's pockets and found $1,500 in cash. He stuffed the money down into his pocket then gave Major Pain the go-ahead nod.

Major Pain screwed the silencer on his .380 as the man continued to beg for his life and fired two quick shots to the head, silencing the man forever.

"Come on, let's get up out of here. Turf wants to see us," Quick said as he headed for his whip.

"Nah, you go ahead without me. I'll catch up with that nigga later. I got something I need to handle real quick." Major Pain gave Quick dap and hopped into his BMW and pulled off.

Quick walked up to the lounge and was immediately met by security. The bouncer was about to search him, but then he realized it was Turf's main man.

"Sorry about that," the bouncer quickly apologized, not wanting to lose his job.

Quick nodded at the big man and entered the lounge. As soon as he stepped inside, the women flocked to him like he was a celebrity.

"Where you in a rush to?" a light-skin joint asked, grabbing Quick's hand.

"Yo, you gon' be right here?" Quick asked, removing his hand from hers.

The woman nodded yes.

"A'ight, bet. I'll be right back," he said as he turned his back on the woman and continued on through the crowd. Quick snaked his way through the crowded lounge as Nikki Minaj's new song blasted through the speakers.

Quick finally made it to the back of the lounge, where Turf and Goliath were posted up talking to a few honeys.

"What's good, slim?" Turf said as he gave Quick dap.

"Chilling." Quick noticed the woman on Turf's arm giving him the what's-good eye. He ignored the woman's hungry look and helped himself to a drink.

"What you think about this place?" Turf said, nodding toward the crowd.

Quick looked at the packed house, full of drunk partygoers. "Shit popping in here tonight," he said.

"I just bought the place," Turf said with a grin. "And I want you to help me run this joint."

Quick gave Turf a disbelieving look. He noticed the girl on Turf's arm still eyeing him. "Word? You bought this whole place?"

"Yeah, it's time to start expanding and building our brand in the streets and in the business world as well," Turf said as he cuffed the woman's ass. "And I think you are a little more business-minded than Major Pain."

"You are so rude," the girl on Turf's arm said. She sucked her teeth. "How you just gon' have a conversation and not introduce me to your friend?"

"My bad. This right here is my new young thing, Tosha," Turf said. "That's my man Quick."

"Nice to meet you, Quick," Tosha said, shaking his hand, looking into his soul.

Before Quick could say another word, some big, steel-face-looking man approached.

"Bitch, what the fuck is you doing over here?" the man yelled. "You suppose to be in the house watching the kids, not out running the mutha-fuckin' streets."

"The kids are at my mother's house!" Tosha yelled back. "What's the big deal?"

The man turned and smacked the shit out of Tosha. "Fuck you mean, what's the big deal?"

Tosha's head snapped back as blood flew from her mouth, and she stumbled back into Turf, who shoved her off of him.

"You just going to sit there and let him hit me like that?" Tosha yelled at Turf, mad 'cause he wasn't protecting her.

Turf waved Tosha off as he continued to sip on his drink and bob his head to the beat that bumped through the speakers.

Embarrassed and with her face throbbing, Tosha lunged toward Turf, but a right hook from Quick dropped her dead in her tracks.

When the man saw his wife hit the floor, he quickly turned and charged toward Quick, running full speed. He tackled Quick like a linebacker, and the two men went crashing to the wet, sticky floor.

Immediately, Turf busted a bottle over the back of the big man's head, forcing Quick to close his eyes as shattered glass showered his face.

Goliath and Turf then went to work on the big man, tearing him up. They stomped him out then watched as security threw the big man and Tosha out like they were trash. Turf and Goliath laughed like nothing ever happened and continued to get their party on.

Quick made his way over to the bathroom, so he could stop the bleeding from his face. He busted in and pushed a nerd-looking man from in front of the mirror, and he began to check his wounds. The glass from the broken bottle had caused minor cuts on his face. He was mad that he didn't get a chance to put in any work on the big man before the bouncers tossed him out of the lounge. He splashed some water on his face then dried it with a paper towel.

Just as Quick was about to exit the bathroom, he heard at least thirty gunshots go off. From how the shots sounded, he could tell that at least three different guns were being fired.

Quick removed his 9 mm from his waistband as he eased out of the bathroom and saw people running for their lives, trying to get out of harm's way. He pushed people out of his way as he tried to make his way toward Turf.

He looked down and saw the big man laid out with a bullet in his head and a machine gun not too far from his hand. On the floor, a few feet away from the big man, was Turf lying in a pool of his own blood, his gun also a few feet away from his hand. And above him stood a crying Goliath. In his hand was an empty Desert Eagle.

Quick made his way over to the scene and saw Turf lying on the floor with a smile on his face. "You a'ight?" he asked, trying not to look at the red spot in the middle of Turf's stomach.

"I'm good," Turf said. "I laid that big nigga the fuck out."

Before Quick could say another word, paramedics came rushing in and rushed him out of the lounge on a stretcher.

Goliath quickly picked up Turf's gun and made a mental note to get rid of it.

"Fuck!" Quick cursed as he watched them wheel Turf out of the lounge on the stretcher.

Major Pain pulled his BMW into the driveway of the house he was looking for. He tucked his .40-cal. into his waistband before stepping out of the car and heading toward the front door. He rang the doorbell and patiently waited for an answer.

Seconds later, he heard a woman's voice yell, "Who is it?" then a series of locks being unlocked.

Nikki opened the door and sucked her teeth when she saw Major Pain standing on the other side of her door. "Fuck you doing here?" she huffed, looking him up and down.

"I just came to apologize," Major Pain said. "And thank you for saving my life."

"Well, you ain't welcome."

The way Major Pain had walked out on Nikki had really hurt her feelings. All she wanted to do was help him out, and all she got in return was a nasty attitude and his ass to kiss.

"How dare you show up to my door after how you treated me, when all I was trying to do was help you out."

"I'm sorry about that," Major Pain told her. "Give me a chance to make it up to you."

"And how do you plan on doing that?" Nikki asked, folding her arms across her chest.

"Can I come inside so we can talk?" Major Pain took a step forward.

Even when Nikki wasn't dressed up, she was still dead sexy. All she had on was a silk robe and a head scarf, and she still looked beautiful.

Nikki reluctantly stepped to the side so Major Pain could enter. Something was telling her not to let him in, but her heart told her otherwise. "You hungry?" she asked as she stepped into the kitchen.

"Yeah. Whip the god up something real quick." Major Pain pulled an already rolled blunt from his pocket and placed fire to the tip. He wasn't used to a woman being nice to him for no reason; they usually had ulterior motives. So when Nikki had saved him that night, he figured she was just helping him in hopes that he would look out for her with some cash.

Nikki placed two plates down on the kitchen table. "You have to eat at the kitchen table around here. I don't allow people to eat in my living room," she told him.

Major Pain helped himself to a seat at the table and saw turkey bacon and pancakes on the plate in front of him. "Yo, good looking," he said with a smile.

"Good looking, my ass," Nikki said, returning his smile. "I'm still mad at you."

Major Pain laughed and the two sat up all night talking and getting to know each other better.

"Jackpot!"

Lucky stood in front of the courthouse, along with Sosa's main girl, Erica. Erica was a well-built, dark-skin chick with a nice body. Not only that, she had a good job. She was a doctor. Erica wore a long, silk-looking weave that came down to the middle of her back, and in the front, she had a neat bang. She wore all black—black jeans, black heels, and a black spandex shirt.

"Damn! What's taking this nigga so long?" Lucky looked down at his watch. He and Erica had been waiting in front of the courthouse for an hour and a half.

Twenty minutes later, Sosa strolled out of the courthouse with his signature bop. "My nigga, what's good?" he said as he gave Lucky dap, followed by a hug. Erica hopped into his arms. "You know they can't keep a good nigga down."

Sosa had been locked up for the past eleven months, and finally, his lawyer had talked the judge into giving him bail.

"Come on, let's make moves from in front of here," Sosa said as the trio hopped into the awaiting Benz truck.

Lucky hopped into the front seat, while Sosa and Erica slid into the back. One of Lucky's young goons drove.

"So what's the plan?" Lucky asked, turning around to face Sosa.

"These crackers got me by the nuts," Sosa said in a disgusted tone. "I only have one option. I have to run."

"You think that would be best?" Erica asked in a concerned tone.

"It's either run or rot in a cell."

"Fuck it! We running then," Erica said.

Sosa looked up at Lucky. "I'ma need you to hold shit down. You the man now," he announced. "Run shit how you see fit, as long as that money keep on flowing in."

"I'm on it." Lucky nodded. It was crazy how shit happened in the hood. Two years ago, when he'd first started working for Sosa, he'd never imagined that Sosa would wind up handing his whole empire over to him.

"When you leaving town?"

"Tonight," Sosa answered. He wasn't sure how shit was going to turn out, but he'd be damned if he just sat around and left his life in the hands of twelve muthafuckas that looked at him like he was an animal. Because that's just what the DA was going to try to make him look like in the jury's eyes.

"Where we heading, baby?" Erica asked.

"Somewhere quiet," Sosa told her, not wanting to reveal where they were going with a car full of people.

The truck pulled up in front of Sosa's mansion, and Erica hopped out and went inside so she could begin packing up their things.

"I'm counting on you to hold me down while I'm gone," Sosa said, looking Lucky in his eyes. "Don't let me down."

"I got you," Lucky said, as he and Sosa slapped hands.

"Do your thing, my nigga. I'll be in touch." Sosa hopped out of the truck and jogged up to the front of his mansion.

Quick and Major Pain stepped onto the hospital elevator and repeatedly pressed for their floor. Both men were silent. Neither could believe that Turf had been shot and was now looking at spending the rest of his life in jail.

Quick stepped off the elevator and headed to the room that had what looked like about a hundred police standing out front.

"Excuse me, officers," Quick said with mock politeness, and he and Major Pain entered the room.

Once inside the room, Quick saw Goliath sitting by Turf's bed. "You a'ight?" Quick asked as he and Major Pain stood over Turf.

"It's not looking too good for me," Turf said, taking a hard swallow. "These muthafuckas trying to throw me under the jail." He nodded toward his wrist that was handcuffed to the bed.

"Damn!" Major Pain shook his head. "Why you ain't just let that shit slide and call me or Quick so we could've handled that shit later for you?"

"Shit happened too fast." A tear strolled down Turf's cheek as he thought back on what had happened. He shed another tear when he thought about his future and the rest of his life behind bars.

Before he could say another word, Detective Davis entered the room. "Well, well, well," he said with a smile. "I see we got the whole gang here today."

"Now ain't the time!" Goliath barked as he shot to his feet.

Detective Davis looked at Goliath and chuckled. "Better sit your big ass down before you get yourself hurt," he said in a serious tone. "Y'all got five minutes to say your good-byes." He then exited the room.

"Fuck him!" Turf looked down at the shit bag attached to his stomach. "Fuck it! Just because I'm out of the game, shit don't stop," he said, looking at Quick. "I want you to take over the operation while I'm down."

"Me?" Quick asked, a surprised look on his face.

"Yeah, you. I know you can do it. Goliath has all the information you need." Turf turned to face Major Pain. "Whatever Quick needs, I want you to back him up."

Major Pain nodded his head, but deep down, he wanted to be the one in control. Not only had he been on the team longer than Quick, but he had also put in way more work than him. But since he wasn't the boss, he decided to bite his tongue.

"You cool with that?" Turf asked, looking into Major Pain's eyes.

"I'm cool with that," Major Pain replied, especially since he didn't have much of a choice.

"Come see me every two weeks, and keep me updated," Turf said, holding out his fist.

"I got you." Quick tapped Turf's fist with his.

Before another word could be said, Detective Davis busted into the room with several other officers on his heels. "Okay, everybody out!" he said.

"Damn! That's fucked up," Major Pain said once the crew was outside. "They trying to throw my man under the jail."

"The show must go on," Goliath said, looking at the two men.

"We having a meeting tomorrow night. Make sure everybody is there." Quick thought about how he was going to handle things now, since Turf was no longer in the picture.

"You need me to do anything tonight?" Major Pain asked.

"Nah, take the night off. See you at the meeting tomorrow," Quick told him as he and Goliath walked off.

"Here." Goliath handed Quick a set of keys, and the two hopped into the Escalade.

Quick looked at the keys in the palm of his hand. "What are these for?"

"Those are the keys to Turf's mansion," Goliath said with a smile. "They yours now."

Quick looked down at the keys and couldn't believe what he was hearing. Not only was he the boss now, but he would also be living like one. Never in a million years did he think this day would come—All decisions made would come from him.

It may have looked like an easy job, but the truth was, Quick didn't even know what he was getting himself into.

"Yo, I need to stop by my crib real quick so we can pick up my girl," Quick said with a smile on his face. He knew Tiffany was going to flip out when she saw the mansion. He couldn't wait to see the look on her face when he surprised her with the good news.

Tommy Gunz and Kat sat parked across the street from Quick's apartment. The two of them had been watching the place for the past four hours.

"Fuck this shit!" Tommy Gunz huffed. "I'm tired of waiting." He reached into the backseat, grabbed his shotgun, and cocked a round into the chamber.

"What you about to do?" Kat asked, a scared look on her face.

When the two came up with the plan, it had sounded simple, but now, when it was time to put in the work, Kat began to get nervous.

"I think we should wait a little while longer," she said.

"Fuck a wait!" Tommy Gunz slid out of the car and tossed his hood over his head. "Get in the driver seat and keep this muthafucka running. I'll be right back," he said. Then he jogged toward the front door, holding the shotgun with two hands.

Tiffany was sitting in the crib watching *Bad Girls Club*, when she thought she heard something tap against the front door.

"What the fuck was that?" she said out loud as she eased her way over to the window and peeked out. She looked out the window for a few seconds and sucked her teeth when she didn't see anything. "Must've been some stupid kids."

She walked back over to the air mattress and sat back down. Before her ass could hit the seat, the front door was blown off the hinges.

Boooom!

Someone busted into the apartment. "On the floor now!" he yelled, aiming the shotgun at her face.

Tiffany heard what the gunman said, but her body was frozen. Her brain was telling her to do what she was told, but her body just wouldn't cooperate.

Tommy Gunz roughly tossed her down to the floor. He then squatted, so she could see his face. "Where it at?" he asked, his breath smelling of tobacco.

"All the money is in my purse." Tiffany pointed to her purse that sat over on the counter.

Tommy Gunz walked over to the counter and snatched up the purse. He emptied everything out onto the floor. He looked down and saw what looked like about five hundred dollars. He smiled. "Oh, you think it's a game?" he said with a smirk on his face as he walked back over to her.

Tiffany knew she was about to get her ass beat, but she refused to just tell the gunman where all Quick's money was. She knew how hard Quick had worked to make that money and she'd be damned if she just gave it up without a fight.

Tommy Gunz snatched Tiffany by her shirt and brought her to her feet, but she quickly turned and punched him in his face.

Tommy Gunz's face didn't budge as a smirk danced on his lips. He threw his head forward with force and head-butted Tiffany, breaking her nose, and blood ran from her nose like a faucet.

Tommy Gunz then grabbed his shotgun with two hands and jabbed her in the stomach, causing her to grab her stomach as she doubled over in pain. "Where it at?" he asked again.

Tiffany looked up at the gunman with a blank expression on her face. The barrel of the shotgun had knocked her out cold.

"Stupid bitch!" Tommy Gunz walked into the back room and opened the closet and found two duffel bags filled with money. "Jackpot!" He tossed both bags over his shoulder.

When Tommy Gunz made his way back into the living room, he saw Tiffany trying to crawl over to her cell phone that was lying over in the pile where all her other belongings were after he had dumped them onto the floor.

Tommy Gunz smiled as he headed for the door. As he reached for the door, he heard a car horn beeping repeatedly. He snatched the door open and saw Quick heading toward the front door with a seven-foot giant on his heels.

Kat sat in the getaway car, nervously looking over both shoulders, hoping that Tommy Gunz would hurry up before someone came and blew up their spot. As she continued to wait, she saw an all black Escalade pull up in front of the apartment Tommy Gunz had entered.

"Awww shit!" she said when she saw Quick hop out of the truck along with a seven-foot monster. Immediately, she began beeping the horn to give Tommy Gunz the heads-up.

Quick and Goliath hopped out of the Escalade and headed for the apartment, until they heard someone beeping their horn like they were crazy.

"What the fuck!" Quick's hand automatically went to his hip as he went to go see who was beeping the horn like they were crazy.

When he got close enough to the car, he saw Kat sitting behind the wheel. He was getting ready to curse Kat out, until he heard Goliath call his name. When he turned around, he saw a hooded man coming from his apartment with what looked like the duffel bags that held all of his money inside.

But that didn't bother him. What bothered him was, the gunman held Tiffany in a choke hold and at the side of her head rested the man's shotgun as the two walked swiftly past them toward the getaway car.

Quick held his gun down at his side as he watched the love of his life walk by him. He made sure he got a good look at the gunman's face as he stopped Goliath from firing his weapon.

"Quick!" Tiffany yelled as the gunman tossed her inside the trunk and slammed it shut.

Tommy Gunz quickly hopped into the passenger seat of the car, and Kat peeled off, leaving the nasty smell of burnt rubber behind.

"Fuck!" Quick watched the taillights of the vehicle disappear into the night. It seemed like every time things appeared to be getting better, they were really getting worse.

"Did you recognize the gunman?" Goliath asked.

"No. But I damn sure recognized the driver," Quick told him.

"What the fuck happened back there?" Kat yelled as she drove through the streets like a madwoman.

"Slow this muthafucka down before you get us knocked," Tommy Gunz growled. He unzipped one of the duffel bags.

When he looked inside, a huge smile appeared across his face. He didn't think taking Quick's money would be this easy, though he knew for sure the end result would be shots fired and, most definitely, a man down. "Easy money."

"I don't know why you smiling," Kat huffed. "He saw both of our faces, genius."

"Look like I give a fuck about that?" Tommy Gunz said seriously. "If you scared, then leave town. With your share of the money, you won't never have to come back." He chuckled.

Kat sucked her teeth. "It's easy for you to say that. Quick's not going to be coming for you, he'll be coming for me. He knows everything about me."

Tommy Gunz ignored Kat as he thought about how he would spend his share of the money. Never in his life had he ever had this much money at one time, so a million thoughts about how he would spend the money swirled around in his brain.

The sound of banging coming from the back of the car interrupted Tommy's thoughts. "Feisty-ass bitch," he mumbled.

Kat continued to drive with a nervous look on her face. She pulled into the garage of Tommy Gunz's grandmother's house, where Tommy Gunz lived in the basement.

Tommy Gunz popped the trunk and aimed his shotgun at Tiffany's head. "Make a peep and you're dead," he said in a calm tone.

"Where the fuck am I?" Tiffany asked, frantically looking around.

"Bitch, didn't he just tell you to shut the fuck up?" Kat barked. She smacked the shit out of Tiffany then placed a strip of duct tape over her mouth, hands, and feet.

Once she was all taped up, Tommy Gunz picked her up and carried her down to the basement while Kat grabbed the two duffel bags and followed him down the steps. Tommy Gunz dropped Tiffany's body onto the floor like a sack of potatoes, and he and Kat sat down at the table and began to count up the money they had just stolen.

The total came up to $150,000.

"Fuck that!" Tommy Gunz said. "Me and you both going to take sixty-five grand apiece and give that bitch-ass nigga Lucky the leftover twenty thousand."

"But we told him forty percent," Kat said, not wanting to cross Lucky. It was because of his info that they were able to pull off the lick.

"I don't give a fuck what we told him," Tommy Gunz said. "How the fuck he gon' know how much was really in the house anyway? That nigga better be glad he's even getting that much."

Kat didn't agree with what Tommy Gunz wanted to do, but her greed forced her to go along with the plan.

"I don't know about you, but I'm leaving town immediately," she said, dumping her share of the money into a book bag and Lucky's share into a shopping bag.

"Scaredy-ass bitch," Tommy Gunz said to himself. He watched Kat quickly pack her money away.

"What you plan on doing with her?" Kat nodded toward Tiffany, whose body lay over in the corner like trash.

"I don't know yet, but I'm sure I'll figure something out," Tommy Gunz replied, an evil smirk on his face.

"Hmm. You play with fire if you want to, not me," Kat said as she walked over to Tommy. "It was nice doing business with you, but I'm out." And the two shook hands, and Kat made her exit.

“Surprise, Surprise”

Major Pain knocked on Nikki’s door and patiently waited for an answer. Seconds later, Nikki came to the door, tears streaming down her face.

“What’s wrong? Why you in here crying?” Major Pain asked, stepping inside the house.

“It’s my brother.” She sobbed. “He’s dead. Somebody killed him.”

“Yo, hold on and slow down for a second.” Major Pain sat Nikki down on the couch. “Calm down and let me know exactly what happened.”

“This guy that my brother used to run with named Lucky just called me,” Nikki said, talking a mile per second. “And he just told me that my brother was murdered, gunned down in the street like an animal.”

Major Pain pulled Nikki in close for a hug. “It’s going to be okay,” he said, rubbing her back gently. Once he heard the name Lucky, his brain automatically went back to the night at the strip club and how Lucky and the man he had just found out was Nikki's brother had jumped him.

"Calm down, baby. Now what I think we should do is go see this Lucky guy and get to the bottom of this. I think he owes you some answers."

"Okay, let me go throw something on real quick." Nikki headed upstairs to the master bedroom.

Once Nikki disappeared upstairs, Major Pain checked the magazine on his .45. Tonight was the night he was going to kill Lucky. Just as he stuck his gun back into his waistband, he felt his cell phone vibrating. "Yo, what up?" he answered.

"Yo, it's me," Quick said into the phone.

From the tone of Quick's voice, Major Pain knew something serious had just happened. "What up?"

"It's Tiffany. Somebody kidnapped her," Quick told him. "I need you to do me a favor."

"Anything you need, I got you," Major Pain told him.

"Keep your eye out for my old girlfriend, Kat. She was the getaway driver. Spread the word. If anybody runs into Kat, grab that bitch and hold her until I get there," Quick said before ending the call.

Major Pain placed his phone back inside its case just as Nikki was coming back down the steps.

"You ready?" she asked.

"Let's do it," Major Pain replied, and the two exited the house.

Lucky stood on the corner talking to a Spanish chick, while beside him, a dice game was going on, and big bucks were being bet. His Benz was parked at the curb, and the sound of Jay-Z was bumping through the speakers. While Lucky got his mack on, he kept looking both ways for any signs of police. Even though he wasn't dirty, he was still on point.

He looked at the Spanish woman who stood in front of him. She wore a pair of black spandex, a black shirt, and some flip-flops, and her hair was wrapped in a neat bun.

"What you doing out here this time of night?" Lucky looked at his watch.

"I'm out here tryin'a see what's up. You be frontin'," the Spanish chick said.

"Yo, you got like five kids, and you never have a babysitter," he said, trying to play her.

"First of all, I only got four kids," she said, like that made such a big difference. "And, second of all, my kids are at my mom's house for the weekend, so you know what that means, right?"

"No. What does that mean?" Lucky asked, not really paying attention to what the Spanish chick was saying. She was just somebody to talk shit with to kill time. Even if her kids were away for the weekend, Lucky hadn't planned on spending time with her.

"That means you got me all to yourself all weekend," the chick said, posing in front of Lucky.

"So you think you ready for a shot at the title?" Lucky licked his lips as he palmed one of the woman's ass cheeks right out in the open.

"I been ready."

Just as Lucky was about to respond, he saw a car pull up a little too close for his liking to the back of his Benz. He was about to go over there, when he saw Kat hop out of the car carrying a shopping bag around her wrist.

Kat stopped directly in front of Lucky. "Yo, I need to talk to you. It's important."

"Damn! Can't you see we was in the middle of a conversation?" The Spanish chick sucked her teeth.

Kat turned and smacked the shit out of her, but the Spanish chick smacked her back, and from there, the two went at it, interrupting the dice game and attracting a crowd.

"Yo, chill," Lucky said as he stepped between the two women.

Other men started yelling, telling Lucky not to break up the fight. The night in the hood was already lively, and as soon as Kat popped up, it got even livelier.

"Bitch, you don't speak unless you spoken to!" Kat yelled as the Spanish girl was being escorted down the block. "And don't think this shit is over with!"

Lucky poured himself a cup of Henny in a five-cent plastic cup. He told Kat, "Yo, don't come over here starting no shit."

"Man, fuck that bitch! I got some real shit I need to talk to you about," Kat said.

"What's on ya mind?" Lucky took a sip from his cup.

"Here's your cut," Kat said, handing Lucky the shopping bag.

Lucky looked down at the bag and immediately knew what time it was. "How did that thing go?" he asked. From how nervous Kat looked, he could tell that something was wrong. He just didn't know what.

"Not good," Kat began. "That muthafucka saw me, and now I don't know what to do."

Lucky shook his head. "Rookies." Honestly, he was surprised that they had even gotten away with the robbery in the first place. "So how can help you?" he asked.

"I need you to protect me."

Lucky laughed in her face. "Help you how?"

"I don't know. I was thinking maybe you could hide me out somewhere."

"Fuck outta here!" Lucky downed the rest of his drink in one gulp. "I'm not hiding you nowhere. If you knew you was going to be scared, then you shouldn't've did what you did," he said coldly. "You better go ask that clown Tommy to protect you, if he ain't already dead."

Lucky knew how his former best friend got down. Quick probably had the whole city out looking for Kat right now, and Lucky wanted nothing to do with that. Just because the two weren't speaking didn't mean that Lucky didn't have love for Quick. He felt bad about giving Kat and Tommy Gunz the info on where to find Tiffany in the first place.

"Damn! So you can't help your girl out?" Kat asked, her face frowned up. "You know what? You a bitch-ass nigga. Don't worry, I'ma have my man come through here and air this whole shit out," she said, feeling embarrassed.

"I know." Lucky poured himself another drink as Kat hopped back into her car.

For the entire ride, Major Pain listened to Nikki cry her eyes out over her brother. He wondered if she even knew what Hawk did for a living. "You a'ight?" he asked, keeping his eyes on the road.

"I'm fine," Nikki replied. "Pull over at the next corner."

Major Pain pulled up and couldn't believe his eyes. Not only did he see Lucky on the corner, but he also saw Kat. The two looked like they seemed to be arguing with each other.

"This must be my lucky day," Major Pain said to himself as Nikki slid out of the car. Just as she got out, Kat hopped into her car and pulled off.

"Fuck!" Major Pain didn't know if he should follow Kat or kill Lucky. After thinking about it for a second, he stepped on the gas and peeled off in pursuit of Kat.

Nikki looked dumbfounded as she watched the BMW pull off in a hurry. "Where the hell is he going?" she thought out loud.

Major Pain made sure he stayed at least three cars behind Kat, so she wouldn't spot him. The whole time he drove, he cursed Kat out as if she could hear him. He was angry at the fact that she had stopped him from getting revenge on Lucky, and now she was going to pay.

Major Pain followed Kat into the parking lot of the Days Inn hotel. "Bum-ass bitch," he mumbled as he pulled out his cell phone and dialed Quick's number.

Kat hopped out of the shower with a frown on her face, still upset about the way Lucky had treated her. While she was in the shower, she was trying to think of a way to make him pay for the way he had treated her. In her mind, she felt that Lucky was supposed to help protect her, since he, too, was in on the job. She didn't know how yet, but before it was all said and done, she was going to make him pay for embarrassing her the way he did.

Just as Kat lay across the bed, she heard a knock at the door.

Knock, knock, knock!

"Go away!" she yelled at the door as she flicked through the channels.

Seconds later, she heard it again.

Knock, knock, knock!

"I said go away!" Kat yelled again with more attitude as she continued to flick through the channels.

Kat's whole body jumped when the door came crashing open. The first person to walk through the door was Major Pain, and he was followed by Goliath.

Kat immediately recognized him as the man who was with Quick when she and Tommy had escaped from Quick's apartment. The last man to enter the room was Quick. The look on his face told her that he wasn't in the mood to play.

"Wait. I can explain," Kat said, standing up. She knew she had fucked up, but still, she tried to talk her way out of it. "He made me do it, I swear."

Major Pain smacked the shit out of her. "Shut the fuck up!" he barked. "When I spotted her, she was with your boy Lucky too," Major Pain announced. "I think he set the whole thing up."

Quick stepped up. "Where's Tiffany?" he asked, his 9 mm hanging down by his side.

"She's with Tommy," Kat said, giving Tommy Gunz up. She didn't want to snitch on Tommy, but her back was against the wall. If it was going to be her or him, she was definitely going to save herself.

"Where can I find this nigga at?" Quick asked.

Earlier that day, Tommy Gunz had called Quick, talking about if he wanted to see Tiffany alive again, then he was going to have to pay another $100,000 to get her back.

"I know exactly where he's at. I'll take you straight to him. Just please don't kill me," Kat begged.

Quick looked over in the corner and saw a book bag filled with money. No longer able to hold his anger in, he turned and smacked Kat across the face with the gun. When her body hit the floor, he immediately began to stomp her head into the floor.

"You gon' steal from me?" he yelled, continuing to stomp away.

Goliath quickly pulled Quick off the woman. "That's enough. We still need her to take us to Tiffany," he reminded him.

"Get her up." Quick walked over to the corner and picked up the book bag filled with his hard-earned money.

Tommy Gunz sat in his basement watching college football. He called himself laying low until the heat died down, so for the past three days, he had been cooped up in his grandmother's basement. He didn't leave that basement for nothing, since he had everything he needed to last him for at least two weeks.

As Tommy watched the game, he heard Tiffany over in the corner moaning. "Bitch, shut the fuck up!" he yelled.

For the past three days, Tiffany lay over in the corner, not able to move. During that time, Tommy didn't feed her anything, nor did he give her anything to drink. When Tiffany had to use the bathroom, she just went on herself. Around the second day, she felt like she had to take a shit. She tried her best to hold it for as long as she could, until she couldn't take it anymore and just shit in her pants like a baby.

Tommy Gunz was sitting on his sofa enjoying the game when he smelled something like shit. "What the fuck!" He hopped up off the sofa and walked over to the corner where Tiffany lay. "Bitch, you shit on yourself?" he yelled. He kneeled down and punched Tiffany in her face. "Nasty-ass bitch!" He pulled out his dick and began to urinate all over Tiffany's head, face, and the rest of her body. "Maybe that will cool you off."

Tommy Gunz laughed as he shook his penis, making sure he got every drop on Tiffany. Before he made it back over to the sofa, he heard somebody knocking on his door. He quickly ran over to the coffee table and grabbed his shotgun before heading for the door.

"Who the fuck is it?" Tommy yelled.

"It's me. Open up."

Immediately, Tommy Gunz recognized Kat's voice. He tossed his shotgun over on the couch as he headed for the door. "Dumb-ass bitch must've changed her mind," he said to himself. He snatched the door open and saw Kat standing on the other side of the door with her face all bruised up.

"Fuck happened to you?" he asked.

Before Kat got a chance to answer, Goliath shoved her out of the way and dropped Tommy with a quick two-piece.

Quick stepped into the basement and immediately spotted Tiffany over in the corner, curled up on the floor like an animal.

While Major Pain and Goliath fucked up Tommy Gunz, Quick was snatching the tape off of Tiffany's mouth. As he touched her, he noticed that she was all wet. At that very moment, he realized that Tommy had pissed on his girl. "You all right?" he asked.

"Yes, baby, I'm fine," Tiffany said, trying to sound strong, but the tears streaming down her face told the truth.

As Quick untied her, he smelled shit. Not wanting to embarrass his woman, he ignored the odor as he helped her up to her feet.

"I helped you out. Now can I go?" Kat asked with a smirk on her face.

Quick looked at her for a second then pulled out his 9 mm, aimed it at her head, and pulled the trigger, dropping her right where she stood. He then turned his 9 mm on Tommy Gunz, who was on his knees, blood streaming from his nostrils.

"Do what you gotta do," Tommy Gunz said, and he closed his eyes.

Quick held the 9 mm to Tommy's head, but instead of pulling the trigger, he handed the gun to Tiffany. "Handle your business, baby," he told her.

Without hesitation, Tiffany took the weapon from him and fired four shots into Tommy Gunz's face.

Quick was surprised at how easily Tiffany shot the man dead like that, but he didn't say anything about it. "Come on, baby, let's get you up outta here." He picked up Tommy's share of the money that they'd stolen from him and helped Tiffany out of the basement.

For the entire ride, Tiffany was quiet. She was just enjoying her freedom and thanking God for letting her make it out of that situation alive.

Goliath pulled up in front of Turf's mansion, leaving Tiffany with a surprised look on her face.

"Surprise!" Quick said.

Quick helped Tiffany out of the truck and inside their new home. Tiffany couldn't believe her eyes as she entered the front door of her new home.

"Is this really our place?" she asked. She had never even seen a house like this, except on TV. "I don't believe it."

"Well, believe it, baby," Quick said, placing a set of keys into the palm of her hand. "This right here is my main man Goliath. He's going to be staying here with us; he's our twenty-four-seven bodyguard."

"Nice to meet you." Tiffany nodded, not wanting to shake the big man's hand 'cause of how filthy she was.

"Go clean yourself up while me and Goliath chat for a second." Quick kissed Tiffany on the lips. He watched as she walked through the big house with a smile on her face. His woman having a smile on her face brought a smile to his face. He knew Tiffany had been through a lot in her life, and he planned on keeping her as happy as possible, so she would never have to think back on her hard times and rough past.

Once Tiffany was out of sight, Goliath asked, "So what you wanna do about that nigga Lucky?"

"Oh, he definitely gonna have to pay for this," Quick said, anger all over his face. "This the second time he tried to take one of my girls out—first Ivy and now this. He definitely gotta go."

"So how you wanna handle this?" Goliath asked, ready to serve his new boss. "You want me to put the word out on the streets?"

"Nah," Quick said. "I'ma have to handle this one myself."

"Guess Who's Back?"

Blake sat on the train with a mean look on his face. He had on his state-issued outfit and boots on his feet. The train was crowded with beautiful women, tourists, and even a few bums, but none of that mattered to him. He had only one thing on his mind—getting revenge on Tiffany. The whole time he was locked away like an animal, the bitch didn't even send him one letter. His birthday had passed three times, and never once did he even get a card. And for that, he was going to make her pay with her life. Especially since it was her fault that he was even in a cage in the first place.

When Blake's stop came, he quickly stepped off the train. He walked down the street on the nice, sunny day, just looking at how much things had changed since he had been away.

A white man snapping pictures bumped into him by accident, and he had to stop himself from beating the white man to death. He still had that jailhouse mentality and so much anger built up inside of him; he was liable to snap any second. Not to mention, he had put on the extra weight and muscle since being locked up. Blake's body was in such good shape and he had so much muscle, he felt he could kill a man with his bare hands if he wanted to.

After walking fifteen blocks, he finally reached the building he was looking for. He entered the building and took the steps to the fourth floor and busted out the staircase without even getting bit winded. He walked down the hall until he reached the door he was looking for and knocked lightly.

Seconds later, a frail-looking older man answered the door, a cigarette dangling from his lips. "Fuck you doing here?" the man asked.

"Uncle Steve, I need to talk to you for a second. Is it all right if I come in for a second?" Blake asked.

Steve stepped to the side so his nephew could enter. "You hungry?" he asked.

"Nah, I'm good," Blake said, standing in the middle of the living room.

"Let me guess—You need some money."

"Nah, I don't need no money."

"Oh," Steve said. "Well, what the fuck you want then?" he asked, wondering why his nephew, whom he hadn't seen in years was standing in his living room.

"I need a gun," Blake said seriously.

Steve laughed loudly. "Is that all?" He pulled a rusty-looking .38 from his back pocket and handed it to Blake.

Blake took the gun and slid it into his pocket.

Steve handed him a box of bullets to go along with the gun. "Let me tell you something," Steve began. "You pull that muthafucka, you better use it. Don't be no pussy, like your father used to be." Then he added, "And another thing; you get caught, and you didn't get the muthafucka from me."

Blake nodded as he headed for the door. "Good looking," he said, and he disappeared out the door. Blake only had one mission on his mind, and that was to kill Tiffany. He didn't care about going back to jail. Until she was gone, he wouldn't be able to rest.

Quick pulled up to the strip club. He'd just got word that Lucky was inside. He parked over in the cut and let the engine die. Then he grabbed his twin 9s from the passenger seat and clutched them tightly as he patiently waited for his former best friend to exit the strip club. Inside, he felt bad about what he was getting ready to do, but his mind was already made up, and he had to do what he had to.

Forty-five minutes later, Quick, a black bandana covering his nose and mouth and a hoodie draped over his head, saw Lucky stumble out of the club with one of his henchmen close by his side. From the way Lucky was walking, Quick could tell he was twisted.

Quick took a deep breath as he hopped out of the stolen car and followed Lucky and his henchman through the parking lot. He walked swiftly in between cars, hoping to cut Lucky and his henchman off.

"Damn! Where the fuck did we park?" Lucky slurred as he and one of his goons stopped in their tracks and searched through the packed parking lot.

Lucky pulled the keys to his Lexus out of his pocket and pressed the alarm. "We right over there," he said once he saw the taillights on his Lexus flash.

As Lucky walked through the parking lot, he heard some footsteps coming from behind him. The footsteps sounded like the person creeping up on them was either running or jogging.

"What the fuck!" Lucky said as he quickly spun around and saw a hooded man jogging toward them in a low hunch.

Before he got a chance to say a word, it was too late. Three shots had already been fired. He tackled his henchman, trying to keep him out of harm's way, but the man already had a bullet in his throat.

"Fuck!" Lucky cursed as he removed the man's .45 from his waistband and sprang up from behind a parked car, firing.

Pow! Pow! Pow! Pow!

Quick ducked behind a parked car as shattered glass showered down onto his head from stray bullets that hit the windows of the car he stood behind. He crept around to the other side of the car and opened fire.

Lucky stayed low, throwing four reckless shots over his shoulder while he zigzagged around the parking lot full of parked cars like it was a maze.

Quick was about to go in for the kill, until people started coming out of the strip club, being nosy. To add to the mix, several different car alarms started going off. "Fuck!" Quick backpedaled over to his stolen ride.

Once the gunshots finished ringing out, Lucky quickly jogged over to his Lexus and stormed out of the parking lot like a bat out of hell.

"Muthafuckas tried to take me out," he said out loud to himself, no longer drunk. Bullets whistling past his head had sobered him right up.

Lucky recognized the hooded man, but he didn't want to believe it. He didn't want to believe that the person he grew up with, the man who was like a brother to him, had just tried to take his life. He didn't want to believe it, but he knew what his eyes saw.

Blake stepped into IHOP and looked around, hoping he saw Tiffany floating around the restaurant.

"How you doing, sir? Can I help you?" the hostess asked politely.

"Yes. Can I speak to the manager please?" he said, still looking around.

Minutes later, Mr. Richardson appeared from the back. "Yes. Can I help you?" he asked, immediately recognizing Blake.

"Yes. Tiffany, where is she?"

"She doesn't work here anymore."

"Do you know where she work at now?"

"No, I don't," Mr. Richardson said. "And if I did, I still wouldn't tell you anyway. Tiffany is a good girl. Why don't you just let her be?"

"Mind your muthafuckin' business before you get hurt." Blake walked out of the restaurant madder than he was when he had first entered.

"In Case You Ain't Know So"

Quick lay across the king-sized bed in his boxers and a wifebeater, watching *Monday Night Football*. On his mind was the incident that went down the other night with Lucky. He could've shot him but missed on purpose. He knew Lucky deserved to die, but he just couldn't do it himself. He didn't have a problem when it came to putting in work, but when it came to putting in work on the person he grew up with, the same person he called his brother, that was a different story.

Tiffany stepped out of the bathroom and cleared her throat, interrupting Quick's thoughts. When Quick looked over, he saw her standing in the doorway of the bathroom wearing nothing but a red thong and a pair of red three-and-a-half-inch pumps.

"Have you been a good boy?" Tiffany purred. She turned the lights down and grabbed the remote to the stereo and cut on some music.

Stevie Wonder's "These Three Words" hummed softly from the speakers as she walked over toward the bed.

Quick tried to get up, but Tiffany pushed him back down on the bed and snatched his boxers off. Before he could even say another word, Tiffany took him into her mouth.

"Shit!" Quick groaned as he sat back and watched his woman go to work on him.

Tiffany used extra saliva to lubricate Quick's dick while she sucked on it just how he liked it, the whole time, looking up at him and bobbing her head a hundred miles an hour and moaning loudly.

When Quick felt himself getting ready to come, he hopped up and pushed Tiffany off of him. "Get ya ass up here on this bed," he demanded, and he watched her crawl onto the bed on all fours. He slid Tiffany's thong to the side, spread her ass cheeks apart, and dove in face-first.

Tiffany moaned loudly as she buried her face into a pillow and gripped the satin sheets as Quick forced her to come for him. He licked and sucked all over her pussy and clit like he needed her come to live. Tiffany kept grinding her ass farther back into Quick's face as he worked his tongue like a lizard, making her come for him yet again.

Just as the two were about to have sex, a loud knock on their bedroom door interrupted them.

"What?" Quick yelled, upset that someone was interrupting his and his baby's quality time.

"It's somebody here that wants to see you!" Goliath yelled from the other side of the door.

Quick hopped up, threw on a wifebeater and some sweat pants, and went to go see what the problem was. "Fuck going on out here?" he said as he trotted down the steps.

When he reached the living room, he saw Lucky and two of his boys being held at gunpoint by a few of his goons.

"This dickhead knocked on the front door," Goliath said. "Didn't want to kill him without checking with you first."

"Were they strapped?" Quick asked, looking Lucky in his eyes.

"Nah," Goliath said. "One of them clowns had a knife on him, but that's about it."

"Speak your piece before I kill you," Quick said, accepting the 9 mm that one of his goons handed him as he stood in front of Lucky.

"I didn't come here for no problems," Lucky said. "I came here to apologize to you again for what happened to Ivy, and I want things to go back to how they used to be."

Quick chuckled. "You can't be serious. You done crossed the line of no return."

"You know me better than anybody," Lucky said. "You know I would never do nothing to hurt you." Lucky knew Quick was still mad at him for killing Ivy, even though it was an accident.

"Plus," Lucky continued, "I was thinking. . . . I got shit on my side on smash, and you seem to be doing pretty good for yourself," he said, looking all around the mansion. "Let's put it all together and shut the town down. Us together and we'll be unstoppable."

"Unstoppable, huh?" Quick said as he thought on it for a second. He knew what Lucky was saying was true, but the question at hand was, could he still trust the man he once called his best friend?

Quick called Goliath over to the side, and the two men spoke in a hushed voice. "What you think?" Quick asked.

"I mean, it sounds good. But can we trust him? is the question," Goliath said. "You have to ask yourself, will the risk be worth the reward?"

Quick turned back around and held his hand out. "Glad to have you back on the team."

Lucky smiled as the two men shook hands then hugged.

"If I even think you trying to pull some funny shit, I will have you dropped like that," Quick said, snapping his fingers.

"Glad to have you back." Goliath gave Lucky a pound.

"We about to shut this whole town down," Lucky said excitedly. "Both of our crews together." He laughed out loud.

Then the three men went into Quick's office, so they could discuss and really get things in order.

Blake walked through the hood wearing all black. The only problem was, it was ninety degrees outside. For the past week and a half, he had been looking for Tiffany and was having no luck. His patience was wearing thin. The longer it took him to find her, the more pain he planned on inflicting on her before killing her.

Blake walked into the building and took the steps to the floor the person he was looking for was on. He bopped down toward the door and knocked with authority.

"Who the fuck is it?" a woman's voice yelled from behind the door.

Blake heard locks being unlocked. Brenda's face looked shocked when she locked eyes with the man on the other side of the door.

"Bitch, don't say a muthafuckin' word!" Blake growled, aiming the .357 in her face as he pushed her back inside the apartment.

"What do you want from me?" Brenda asked, looking nervous.

Blake roughly shoved her down onto the couch and aimed his pistol right between her eyes. "Where is Tiffany?"

"I don't know," Brenda said. "I haven't spoken to that girl in months."

Just as the words left Brenda's mouth, the .357 made contact with the side of her face. "You must think I'm playing," Blake said in a calm tone as he hopped on top of her and began beating her face in with his weapon.

Brenda couldn't take the pain anymore and gave in. "Okay, okay, okay!" she yelled. "I'll tell you where she lives."

Once Blake got all the information he needed out of Brenda, he put a bullet into her head and walked back out the door like nothing had ever happened.

"Nah, I don't know about this," Major Pain said to Quick, his eyes locked on Lucky. He felt the man couldn't be trusted and only wanted to be back on the team because his and Sosa's empire was now crumbling right before their eyes. "How we know we can trust this muthafucka?"

"The only reason I left the first time was because Turf was trying to feed me table scraps," Lucky announced. "I'm not gon' just sit around and let somebody play with my paper. Things are different now though. We bringing two strong teams together as one, and I promise y'all, all of our pockets will only get fatter."

Before Major Pain got a chance to reply, Quick said, "We going to work this shit out, and we all gon' get this money."

The little get-together that Quick and Tiffany threw inside the mansion looked more like a party than anything else. There was liquor, and women, and men all over the place.

"Tonight, I want you two to enjoy y'all selves," Quick said. "We are all a team now, and the faster we start acting like it, the faster we will all become millionaires," he told them, as Tiffany crept up on him from behind and wrapped her arms around his waist.

"Can I borrow you for a second?" Tiffany slurred with glassy eyes.

Just from looking at her face, Quick could tell she was twisted.

"What's up, baby?" Quick kissed her on the lips as the two walked over toward the bar area.

Tonight, the two just wanted to celebrate all the things they had overcome. Not to mention, it was their four-year anniversary, though the two weren't married. Yet.

Quick and Tiffany were loving the fact that they didn't have to want for anything ever again; it felt good, especially for two people who weren't used to having shit.

"Can I get some of your time tonight please?" Tiffany purred as she poured herself and Quick a glass of vodka each.

"Chill. I need some juice in my shit." Quick added a bit of orange juice to his glass. He could drink it straight if he wanted to, but he had nothing to prove. "You looking good tonight," he said, palming her ass.

"How good?" Tiffany asked with a seductive smile on her face.

"Good enough to eat," he whispered in her ear. Quick made sure he took her ear into his mouth before he pulled his face away.

"Sometimes I look at you and just say to myself, you are too good to be true," Tiffany said seriously. "This all feels like a dream to me. Some days, I just be praying that if this is a dream that I never have to wake up."

Quick took a sip from his drink as he listened to what Tiffany was saying. He knew that Tiffany really loved him for him, and he also knew that she was as loyal as they came. Nowadays, you couldn't find a person who you could believe, let alone trust.

He pulled Tiffany in close to him. "This ain't no dream. All the love I got for you is real, and you have nothing to worry about 'cause I'm not going anywhere. You never have to be alone again."

"I trust you." Tiffany grabbed Quick's hand and led him upstairs to their bedroom.

"What about our guests?" Quick asked.

"They'll be all right." Tiffany smirked as they entered the bedroom.

Quick finished his drink as he watched her step out onto the balcony in their room, from where she smiled and motioned with her finger for him to join her.

Blake pulled up to the address that Brenda had given him, and instantly, he knew he had to be at the wrong address. There was no way this could be the right address. He looked out of his window and saw a huge house that looked like a mansion, and outside, they seemed to be having some type of party, with cars parked all over the place.

"Fuck!" Blake banged on the steering wheel, pissed that Brenda had given him the wrong address. If she were still alive, he definitely would've paid her another visit for wasting his time.

Just as he was about to pull off, he saw a woman who looked like Tiffany step out onto the balcony. As he looked closer, he saw that the woman up on the balcony was indeed Tiffany. It turned out that Brenda had given him the real address after all.

"Damn!" Blake said to himself. He noticed that Tiffany still looked good, even after all these years, and he found himself still attracted to the woman.

As good as she looked, Blake still had to do what he had to do. But the more he looked at Tiffany, the more he thought about not killing her. "I'll just beat her ass real good. Then we can start over fresh," he told himself.

Seconds later, Blake's face frowned up when he saw a man join her on the balcony. "What the fuck!" he yelled as he recognized the man on the balcony. He watched as Quick and Tiffany kissed out on the balcony and their hands explored each other's bodies. The sight was enough to make Blake throw up. He continued to watch as Quick stripped Tiffany of all her clothes, before his head disappeared.

Blake's fist balled up as he watched Tiffany's head go back in pleasure. He couldn't see her facial expression, but from her body language, she seemed to be enjoying the way Quick was pleasing her.

Minutes later, Quick's head rose from down below and was back in plain view. Blake shook his head in disgust as he watched Quick turn Tiffany around and bend her over. It looked as if Tiffany was looking directly at him as Quick penetrated her from behind. He watched as Quick forcefully thrust himself in and out of Tiffany repeatedly.

From Tiffany's facial expression, she seemed to be loving every minute of it. After Quick finished pounding Tiffany out, she slowly slid down to her knees and sucked on her man's dick until he filled her mouth with his juices. Tiffany swallowed it all and came up with a smile on her face, and she and Quick went back inside.

Blake couldn't believe what he'd just witnessed. All thoughts of sparing Tiffany's life were now out the window. And once again, the only thing on his mind was murder.

“You Already Know”

The next morning, Tiffany came downstairs and just shook her head at the trash and empty cups all over the place. She saw Quick ’sleep on one couch, Major Pain ’sleep on another couch, and Goliath lay stretched out on the floor. Over in the corner lay four women who were too drunk to make it home. Tiffany ignored all the bodies that were sound asleep as she began to clean up.

Quick heard a slight noise and opened his eyes to investigate. When he saw Tiffany cleaning up, he relaxed a bit. “Hey, baby,” he said, joining her in the spacious kitchen.

“Get y’all lazy asses up,” Tiffany joked. “I’ma make a nice, big breakfast.”

“That’s what I’m talking about,” Quick said. He knew Tiffany could cook her ass off.

Tiffany opened the fridge and sucked her teeth. “Damn! Ain’t shit up in here.”

“You want me to drive you to the supermarket?” Quick offered.

"Nah, I got it," Tiffany replied. "You just sit down and relax yourself and let your woman handle this." She winked as she went upstairs to get dressed.

Ten minutes later, she returned downstairs wearing a pair of black stretch pants, a wife-beater, and on her feet, some open-toe sandals. She just threw her hair into a loose ponytail, and on her face, she sported a pair of dark Chanel shades. "I'll be back in a few," she yelled over her shoulder as she walked out the door.

As soon as she stepped outside, she noticed red cups strewn all over the lawn. "You see, this is why you can't invite niggas to shit," she huffed. She stuck her head back inside the door. "Baby, can you get these cups up from off the lawn please? Thanks. I love you," she said, not waiting for a reply as she headed out.

A block away, Blake sat inside his hooptie watching Tiffany's every move. "I got you now, you unloyal bitch!" he growled as he watched Tiffany hop into her Lexus and pull off. "And you out here eating good while I was locked up and didn't send me a dime," he said out loud as he followed the Lexus.

The entire time he drove, scenes from Tiffany and Quick having sex up on the balcony last ight kept flashing through his brain. The more e thought about how Tiffany had betrayed him, he angrier he became.

Blake followed Tiffany's Lexus into the super- narket parking lot and watched her every move. Ie wanted to hop out of his car and blow her rains all over the sidewalk, but he decided he vould wait and make his move when she exited he supermarket. Once he was sure she was nside the store, he parked his hooptie right next o the Lexus.

Blake slid out of the hooptie with a slim jim nd a screwdriver in his hand. Before he slid he slim jim down above the lock, he decided o check the door first, and to his surprise, it vas open. "Dumb-ass bitch," he mumbled as he ulled the .38 from his waistband and ducked lown into the backseat of the Lexus.

Tiffany stood in the express line waiting for he cashier to ring up her stuff. The lady in front f her didn't have enough money to pay for all of er groceries, so she was trying to decide what he wanted to put back.

The cashier sucked her teeth and rolled her yes at the woman for holding up the line. She vas getting ready to say something, until Tiffany poke up for the woman.

"Miss, you don't have to put nothing back," Tiffany said politely. "Ring our shit up together, please," she said to the cashier. "Oh, and give us separate bags please," she added, humiliating the cashier the way she had just tried to do to the woman.

"Thank you so much," the woman said as she grabbed her groceries and exited the store.

Tiffany shook her head. She never understood why people who didn't like people always seemed to have a cashier or customer service job. If they didn't like or want to be bothered with people, why didn't they apply for jobs where they didn't have to deal with people? She shrugged it off as she walked through the parking lot.

She pressed a button on her keychain, and instantly, the trunk popped open. She tossed the groceries into the trunk, walked around to the driver's side of the car, and slid into the front seat. Just as she was about to place the car into drive, she felt a cold barrel on the nape of her neck.

"I know you didn't think your daddy would forget about you, now did you?"

Immediately, Tiffany recognized the voice. Her eyes widened as she saw Blake's face through the rearview mirror. Right then and there, she knew today was the day she was going to die.

“I don’t know how many times I have to keep elling you,” Blake said through clenched teeth. You belong to me.”

“What do you want from me?” Tiffany asked, lisgust in her tone. Usually, she would’ve been rying right now, but times had changed. Now, he was thinking about how she could kill Blake.

“Bitch, just shut the fuck up and drive.” Blake hoved the barrel of his gun farther into the back of Tiffany’s neck.

Tiffany cursed herself for leaving her doors pen. Blake had been gone for so long, she had orgotten about him and tried to block him out of her mind, making it like he never existed. But now, he was back and in the flesh.

From the look in his eyes, Tiffany knew Blake vas planning on killing her. If she was going to nake a move, she was going to have to do it fast.

“You out here fuckin’ and living the good life vhile I was stuck in a fuckin’ cell!” Blake yelled. He hit Tiffany on the side of her head with the gun, causing her head to bounce off the driver’s side window.

“Fuck you!” Tiffany capped back. “Quick is nore of a man than you will ever be.”

Whack!

That last remark caused her to get hit with the gun again.

"Fuck you and that bitch-ass nigga Quick!" Blake laughed. "After I kill you, I got something special planned for that clown."

Tiffany hopped onto the highway and gunned the engine. If she was going to make a move, it was going to have to be now.

"Bitch, what the fuck is you doing?" Blake yelled nervously as the Lexus sped up. "Slow this muthafucka down before I blow your brains out!"

Tiffany took a deep breath as she quickly reached behind her and grabbed the gun. The Lexus swerved back and forth as the two fought for control of the gun. She tried to steer with one hand as she struggled for the gun with her other hand.

Blake won the battle and gained control of the gun, but before he even got a chance to aim it at Tiffany's head, she stomped on the brakes, causing him to go flying through the windshield.

Tiffany held on to the steering wheel with two hands, trying to give her nerves a second to calm down. She looked in the middle of the highway and saw Blake laid out motionless on the ground. Then she peeked into the rearview mirror and saw that several accidents had occurred because of her hitting her brakes the way she had.

"Ma'am, are you okay?" a white man asked, standing at the driver's window of Tiffany's car.

Tiffany didn't respond. She just nodded her head as she heard the sound of several sirens. The only thing going through her mind was, she needed to get back to Quick so he could protect her. She stepped on the gas and swerved around Blake's body as she headed back home.

Just as Tiffany made it about three blocks away from her house, she saw flashing lights in her rearview mirror.

"Fuck y'all," she said to herself as she kept on driving. She wasn't going to stop until she made it home. She knew she was in trouble, but she felt safer in the presence of her man. Besides, she didn't trust the police, especially not with her life.

After about a three-minute high-speed chase, she pulled up on the front lawn of the mansion, prepared to deal with whatever came her way.

“Fuck the Police”

Quick and Lucky stood in front of the mansion, alling themselves cleaning up after the house uests, but really, they were putting together plan on what the next move was going to be. 'he two men had put their differences aside and lanned on making the best out of it.

Before Quick could say another word, he saw 'iffany's Lexus pull up to the front lawn with a ig-ass hole in the front windshield.

“What the fuck!” he said out loud.

Tiffany hopped out of the front seat and tarted running toward him and Lucky, but efore she could cover a few feet, a white officer oughly tackled her to the ground.

“Didn't I tell you to stop running?” The officer unched Tiffany in the face then pulled out a pair f handcuffs.

Quick and Lucky were all over the officer before e even got a chance to put the cuffs on even one f Tiffany's wrists, attacking and assaulting him,

really stomping him out until he was no longe
moving.

"You all right?" Quick asked as he helpe
Tiffany up to her feet.

"Blake is out of jail," Tiffany said, out of breath
"He tried to kill me."

Just as Tiffany got the words out of her mouth
six cars pulled to a screeching stop in front of th
mansion.

"Let's go inside," Quick said in a hurried voice
and he, Tiffany, and Lucky ran inside.

"Everything all right?" Goliath asked as h
and Major Pain sat on the couch with the ladies

"Cops outside," Lucky announced.

"What happened?" Quick asked, looking a
Tiffany.

"I went to the store to get us some breakfas
and Blake crept up on me and tried to kill me
Long story short, I think I killed him instead.
can't go to jail," she said, a worried look on he
face.

"Don't worry, baby. Ain't nobody going to jail,
Quick told her. "Go upstairs and fill as many bag
as you can with money, and hurry up!" he said a
he watched Tiffany run up the steps. "I don't wan
to get y'all niggas involved, so y'all can leave ou
through the back door."

"Fuck that! We all a family," Lucky said
loading up an UZI.

"I got warrants, so you already know how I'm going out," Major Pain said with a smirk on his face.

Goliath smiled as he turned and looked over at the ladies. "Y'all bitches get the fuck out!" He smacked one of the ladies on her ass as she was leaving.

Tiffany came downstairs carrying two duffel bags full of money. "I'm ready."

"I need y'all to cover us." Quick reached into his gun closet and pulled out two TEC-9s. "Cover us, and when we make our move, y'all can make y'all's escape out through the back." He gave each man a hug, before he and Tiffany headed over toward the garage.

"Let's do it," Major Pain said, and he opened the door and stuck his M-16 out and held on to the trigger as he watched the police scatter for cover as bullets rained.

Seconds later, the police returned fire. Major Pain smiled as he took cover and reloaded.

Lucky stuck his UZI out the door and let it rip. He hated the police and tried to take out as many as he could.

Once he took cover, Major Pain stuck his arm out the door and squeezed the trigger, and the assault rifle rattled in his hand.

Just as Goliath went toward the door to get into the gunfight, a bullet ripped through his thigh. "Awwww shit!" the big man growled. But he still cocked round after round into his shotgun and let it rip.

When Quick and Tiffany reached the garage, gunshots could be heard echoing throughout the hallway, followed by the sound of machine gun bursts. "Come on, we gotta go," he said.

"I'm so sorry, baby," she said as she hugged Quick tightly. Then she tossed the bags onto the backseat of the all-black BMW.

"We gotta go, baby," Quick said as he hopped behind the wheel and waited for Tiffany to join him.

Seconds later, Quick drove straight through the garage door, gaining the attention of every officer that stood outside.

"Come on, you pussies!" he yelled as he swerved into the street on the other side of the mansion. That move gave him and Tiffany about a two-to-three-minute head start.

Once Major Pain heard Quick make his exit, he dropped his M-16. "Come on, we gotta go," he said, and the three men quickly made their way over to the back door. "You gon' be all right?" he asked, looking down at Goliath's leg.

Goliath gave him a crazy look. “C’mon. You know it’s going to take more than a punk-ass shot to my leg to stop the god.”

Major Pain looked over at Lucky and gave him a hug. “Be safe,” he said.

“You already know,” Lucky replied. “Let’s all meet up at the strip club down in the Bronx that we always used to go to.”

The three men all shook hands and split up.

Quick tried to drive down backstreets to dodge the cops, but it was no use. It seemed like every cop on the force was after them.

“I’ma pull over and bang out with these pigs,” he said, peeking in his rearview mirror. “That will give you enough time to get away.”

“No, I’m not leaving you,” Tiffany said sternly. There was no way she was going to just leave her man for dead by himself.

“Don’t be stupid. You belong on a island somewhere, enjoying that money or—”

“No!” Tiffany said, cutting him off. “I belong to you!”

Just as Quick was about to reply, he felt a cop bump him from behind, and four shots came crashing through the back windshield.

"Put your head down!" Quick yelled as he made a sharp right turn, causing the BMW to fishtail a little.

Tiffany reached into the backseat for one of the TEC-9s and shot through the back window, returning fire, getting the police off their ass.

"Get down, baby, and keep your head down," Quick said, weaving in and out of traffic.

As Quick drove, he noticed a few Good Samaritans on the road trying to help the police box them in. "Move, muthafuckas!" he yelled, and he rammed one of the cars from behind.

Then suddenly, one of his back tires got shot out.

"Fuck! Grab that money and a gun," he said as he grabbed one of the TEC-9s and stopped the car. "We can't stay in this car." Quick hopped out and opened fire on the police, and Tiffany ran inside a sleazy-looking bar.

Once Quick ran out of bullets, he quickly joined Tiffany inside the bar.

"Everybody, out right now!" Quick yelled, and the few people who were in the bar scampered without having to be told twice.

"We are fucked," Quick said, looking over at Tiffany, who had a worried look on her face. "Fuck it!" he said in a defeated tone. "I'm going out the front door. I want you to take that money and go out the back door and never look back."

"Fuck no!" Tiffany yelled. "If you go out that front door, then I'm going with you."

"This ain't for you," Quick said, looking in her eyes. "You don't belong here," he whispered as he kissed her.

Tiffany kissed him back and replied, "I belong to you, and don't you ever forget that."

Quick smiled. Never in his life did he ever expect the waitress he had met a while back at IHOP to be his soul mate. "I don't know what I would do without you," he said.

"You never have to find out." Tiffany smiled, but her eyes told him that she was scared and nervous.

Quick grabbed her hands and held them tightly, and he said a quick prayer.

"Amen," he said when he was done, and he and Tiffany hugged tightly.

"I love you," Tiffany whispered, her eyes closed.

"Go out that back door please," Quick begged. "Please."

"Sorry. No can do. You stuck with me." She smiled then kissed him one more time.

"Fuck it!" Quick said as he walked over to the bar and poured himself and Tiffany a shot. "To us," he said, and he raised his glass.

"To us," Tiffany repeated, and the two touched glasses then downed the liquor in one gulp.

Quick grabbed his TEC-9 and placed a fresh clip into the base and headed toward the front door. "I love you," he said, and he snatched the front door open and ran out firing.

Tiffany was right on his heels, following her man's lead, shooting at anything moving. Five seconds hadn't even passed before the police dropped both Quick and Tiffany right out in the middle of the street, riddling their bodies with bullets. More bullets than necessary.

Tiffany's body dropped and landed right next to Quick's, and the two lay side by side, looking up at the sky, the two of them finally free.

Detective Davis looked down at Quick's and Tiffany's bodies and just shook his head. He hated locking people up, but he preferred them in jail than dead any day. He said a silent prayer for the two before walking off, leaving them to rest.

"I Don't Think So"

Blake sat on his couch watching *Jerry Springer*, his face badly scarred from flying through the front window, and he also had a broken leg. He had heard the news about Quick and Tiffany's murder and didn't feel sorry for the couple, not one bit. He felt they got exactly what they deserved. He was still a little upset, because he wanted the joy of watching Tiffany beg him for her life before he killed her, but once again, she had outsmarted him and got away.

"Stupid muthafuckas," Blake said out loud, shaking his head at the thought. He leaned over to grab the remote, when suddenly, his front door was kicked in.

Blam!

"What the fuck!"

"You look surprised to see us," Lucky said.

Lucky smiled as he and Major Pain stood side by side, both men wearing all black, including black leather gloves. And in each man's hand was a .45 handgun.

"Hey, brothers. What's this all about?" Blake asked with a weak and nervous grin.

"Quick and Tiffany send their regards," Lucky said, and he and Major Pain filled Blake's body with holes and left him lying dead on his living room floor like the trash he was.

"Now they can finally rest in peace," Major Pain said, and he and Lucky exited the raggedy apartment.

Coming Soon

March 2015

Obession 3:

Bitter Taste of Revenge

Chapter One

"Oh my God! Somebody please help me. I can't have my baby born in this place." Secret was curled up into a tight fetal position. She looked as though she was inside of her own mother's womb instead of a mother about to push a baby out of hers.

Her knees were rammed into the bottom of her protruding belly. Her toes were pointed stiff, more so than a ballerina performing the Nutcracker. Her arms were clinched tightly around her stomach. She was going to keep that baby inside of her at all costs.

"Urghhhh!" she cried out as another sharp pain cut through her midsection.

"Will somebody come help this bitch please? Ain't nobody got time for this shit. A nigga tryin'a sleep. Damn!"

Secret's cellmate showed no empathy for the excruciating pain she had been going through since lights out. Secret couldn't have cared less though. She didn't need empathy. She needed someone to come in with a great big needle or a pill potent enough to take all this pain away . . . without harming her baby of course.

Secret had suffered enough pain in her short nineteen years for both herself and her unborn baby. She never wanted her daughter to live the painful life she had. There were plenty of nights she just lay on her jail cot, held her stomach, and stared up at the ceiling, praying to God that her baby would skip the generational curse of the Miller family. It was a curse that included a miserable life, with miserable parents, being raised in the streets of Flint, Michigan.

Within that prayer, Secret always told God, "And please don't let it be a girl." There had been Secret's grandmother, who Secret's mother, Yolanda, had sworn was the worst mother in the world. Secret begged to differ, not because the grandmother she knew had been as sweet as pumpkin pie, but because Secret felt that Yolanda was the worst mother in the world. In her defense, Yolanda said her own mother had made her that way. Would Secret be using that same excuse years from now for her own daughter? And then, would her own daughter be using it for her own daughter, and so on?

Tears would slide out of Secret's eyes and onto her paper-thin pillow at just the thought of having a girl child. The women in her family, all having had children in their teens, hadn't made things any better. It had only made the struggle of raising a child worse. Secret just knew for sure if she had a boy, the curse would end there. Not only that, but she felt that a boy would have a better chance of surviving the streets of Flint. It seemed no matter how hard Secret tried, she was never going to be able to escape the city. She'd been born and raised in those streets and it definitely looked like her child was about to be as well.

"Owwwwweee. Jesus!" A strong cramp ripped through Secret's lower abdomen. They were coming with vengeance in what seemed like every five minutes now.

At first the cramps that woke Secret up out of her sleep were bearable. They weren't any worse than bad menstrual cramps. As a matter of fact, when the cramping first started, Secret was able to close her eyes again and sleep through it. But that was when they were minor and only about an hour apart. Through the night, they had gotten stronger and closer together.

Secret couldn't take it anymore. She had waited this thing out as much as she could. She had lay there and tried to hold that baby inside of her so that it wouldn't come into this world with the stigma of being born inside a jailhouse. The baby was in control now and it was coming out whether Secret liked it or not.

With sweat pouring from her body, her gown sticking to her like toilet paper, Secret managed to sit up on the edge of the cot on her top bunk. "God help me," she repeated three times. She breathed in and out deeply. She took her hand and wiped her forehead to keep the salty sweat from rolling into her eyes and stinging them. Her hair was drenched and matted. There was no combing that mess out. She'd have to get it shaved, she just knew it. But this was no time to be concerned about hair care. She had to get out of that bed and go over to the door and yell for help. Her lazy cellmate sure wasn't getting out of her bed to do it.

Just as Secret was about to hop down, another cramp ripped through her. At the same time, it felt like her insides had fallen out. She let out the loudest roar ever.

Her cellmate, who'd had her pillow over her head, snatched it off. She leaned her head from out under the bunk to yell at Secret for making such a ruckus. "Will you shut the fuck—"

The gushing water that poured from the top bunk halted her cellmate's words.

"What the fuck?" Her cellmate jumped up. "Did this bitch just fuckin' piss on me?" she asked, wiping the moisture that had hit her face. She then looked down at her wet hands. "I'm 'bout to fuck this bitch up!"

She got up from the bottom bunk and went right for Secret's jugular. Before she could do any real damage to Secret, the cell door flung open and two guards came storming in.

"What the hell is going on in here?" the female guard asked.

"Looks like Mel is trying to get some of that pregnant pussy," the male guard said and laughed.

Mel, Secret's cellmate, had spread Secret's legs apart, not to try to have sex with her, but to have a better position at putting her hands around her throat. She'd had every intention of choking the life, and the baby, out of her cellmate, hadn't the guards shown up.

"Pregnant pussy is the best," the female guard agreed.

"How the fuck you know?" he asked his co-worker.

She only winked and smiled.

"Nasty ass dyke," he said under his breath a
they both went over, taking their own sweet tim
to get Mel off of Secret.

"No, fuck that!" Mel resisted as the two guard
subdued her. "That bitch pissed on me."

"Aww, poor baby," the female guard teased
"And since when don't you like a little golde
shower?"

The two guards hollered out in laughter as Se
cret hollered out in pain. This made the guard
turn their attention to Secret.

"Oh, shit!" the female guard yelled out whe
she saw the condition Secret was in.

Secret was sitting on the edge of the be
with her legs cocked open. She was drenched
clutching her belly and clearly in pain.

"I think she's in labor," the female guard said

"Hel . . . hel . . . help me," Secret manage
to pant out. "My baby. My baby." The tear
wouldn't stop flowing.

"Help me get her down," the male guard sai
as he pulled out his walkie talkie. He manage
to help the female guard get Secret down as h
called in the situation. "We have an inmate going
into labor. Looks like the baby could be born
any minute. Give the infirmary the heads-up.
Prepare for her arrival in five." He ended the
conversation, put the device away, and was now

able to fully assist with getting Secret out of the cell. Once they got Secret through the threshold, they closed and locked the cell back up.

On one side of the door, Secret was screaming her head off. On the other side, Mel was lying back down on her cot, saying, “Good, now a nigga can finally get some sleep.”

Secret’s screams echoed off the walls of the corridors as the guards half carried–half forced her to walk to the infirmary. For Secret, the five-minute trek felt like a walk to death row instead of the hospital bed that was waiting for her once the guards carried her into the cold room. The immediate, what felt like, glazier temperatures, hitting Secret’s wet skin was sure to cause her pneumonia. But catching a cold to the tenth degree wasn’t of importance right now, but getting that baby from between her legs without incident was.

“How far apart are your contractions?” Secret heard the voice of the female doctor ask her.

Secret had placed the corner of a sheet into her mouth and was biting down on it as a contraction hit her hard. She couldn’t have answered the doctor if she’d wanted to. She didn’t want to. There was no time for 101 questions. Her water had broken. Her contractions felt like they were coming every second.

The hell with questions; just get this baby out of me! Secret screamed in her mind.

"Damn it! Will you answer the doctor? She's trying to help your ass!" The female correction officer spoke more out of fear than anger. She'd never been in this situation before and didn't know what to do. Secret looked more like she was about to die than give birth.

"I can take it from here," the doctor looked at the female correction officer and said. She didn't want the CO's negative and nervous energy making things worse for her patient.

The female CO just stood there frozen, stunned by the excruciating pain the young woman was somehow able to endure. The doctor's words hadn't been able to melt the ice.

"I said I can take it from here." This time, the doctor's tone was sterner and she looked at the male CO, signaling for him to get his partner and go.

He, too, had been mesmerized by the whole idea that Secret was about to give birth to a live human being. Having no children of his own, no baby momma to stand beside in the delivery room, he'd never experienced anything like this either. He wasn't frozen in fear, though, like his counterpart. He was more in awe. He did, in fact, acknowledge the doctor's words. He pulled his attention away from Secret and looked at the doctor. "Oh, okay." He looked back to Secret while tugging his coworker's arm. "Come on. Let's go."

The female CO, feeling his hand on her arm, was able to snap out of her trance. She looked from her coworker to Secret as he slowly began to pull her away.

The doctor was doing all she could not to yell, "Get the fuck out already!" She turned her attention back to Secret as the two COs exited the room. "I need you to work with me here, Secret, so that I can help you." The doctor had seen Secret before, so she knew her name. She'd given her a check-up or two during Secret's past month of incarceration. "Can you do that for me?"

Secret nodded vigorously. She'd do anything she needed to do for help right now.

"I need you to turn over onto your back. Okay?"

Secret had been most comfortable, for lack of a better word, lying balled up on her side. If lying on her back meant the doctor could do something to help the pain go away, she was more than willing to change positions. If she could.

Upon seeing Secret attempt to turn onto her back, the doctor immediately began to assist her. Secret moaned and groaned with every movement.

"It's okay. I know it hurts. I know it hurts," the doctor consoled. Once she had Secret on her back, she took some plastic gloves out of the pockets of her white jacket and placed them on her hands. She spread Secret's legs open just as a contraction hit. The doctor's eyes nearly bulged out of her head. This wasn't her first time at the rodeo, but it was the first time an inmate had been this far along before being brought in for help. "Okay, Secret. Grab onto the rail of the bed and squeeze it whenever the pain shoots through, but don't push. Not yet."

The doctor walked over to the phone on the wall and picked it up. She hit a couple of numbers and then began talking. "Where are you? I need your assistance. I have an inmate down in the infirmary. She's in labor." There was a pause, and then the doctor yelled, "I don't give a shit about you giving an inmate with a migraine some damn pills. Did you hear what I said? This inmate is about to have a baby! Get your ass back here now if you want your job when you do decide to return!" The doctor slammed the phone down and mumbled under her breath,

Giving an inmate with a migraine some pills, ny ass. More like giving an inmate some head."

Secret was in far too much pain to make out vhat the doctor was fussing about. She just did ıs she was told, clinching the bars on the bed for lear life.

When the doctor returned to Secret's bedside, she had two cold, wet white towels. She placed one on Secret's forehead and another on her ıeck. She then went back to the foot of the bed :o continue checking Secret out. "Secret, I'm just going to slide your underwear off." The doctor slid Secret's drenched panties off and then laid them on a silver rolling tray that was only about a foot away. She used her gloved hands to gently spread Secret's legs apart. She inserted her fingers into Secret, to best guess how much Secret had dilated. A few seconds later, she closed Secret's legs, pulled her gown down, and walked back over to the phone while removing her gloves and pitching them into the trash.

Just as the doctor started talking to someone on the phone, the worst contraction ever hit Secret. It made her upper body rise and a curdling howl escaped her throat.

The doctor hung up the phone and walked back over to Secret's bedside. She spoke as calmly as she could. "Secret, your water has broken and you are fully dilated. I could feel the baby's head." Actually, she could see it, but she didn't want to freak Secret out too badly. "Nurse Caine was assisting another inmate but is on her way down to help me." She grabbed Secret's hand. "I called for help for you to be transferred to the hospital, but honey, this baby is coming and is going to be born here."

Secret grabbed the doctor's hand and squeezed it almost as tightly as she had been squeezing that rail just a few minutes ago. "No," Secret said with both passion and authority intertwined. "I cannot have my baby in this jail." Tears poured from Secret's eyes. "Please don't make my baby have to live with that its whole life. Please, Doctor. Wait for the ambulance and let me have my baby in a real hospital like a mother should."

"Secret, I can't—"

Secret cut her off by squeezing the doctor's hand with her other hand as well. She was pleading like a prisoner being held captive, begging for freedom. "Please, Doctor. I can't have my baby in jail. I'd rather die. I'd rather it die." The tears continued to stream. She trembled. A contraction hit her, but she clamped her teeth together to bear the pain. Only the doctor telling her what she wanted to hear would give her peace of mind.

"This baby is not going to wait, honey. There is nothing I can do," the doctor told her. "It's not really up to me. That baby is coming when it's ready. Now, I have to get you prepped so I can assist your little one." The doctor eagerly went to walk away. Not only did she need to help bring Secret's baby into the world, but she could no longer stand to look into Secret's eyes. There was too much desperation and pain for her to witness.

"No, please." Secret refused to let go of the doctor's hands. "Don't do this to me." Secret shook her head back and forth.

The doctor had no idea what was going through her patient's head, but she could only imagine. Who wanted their child to walk around for the rest of their lives with the stigma attached of being born in jail? But her hands were tied. It was in God's hands. He was the one who decided when a life would come into the world. She was just there to help.

The doctor leaned down close to Secret. "I understand how you feel, I really do. But if I don't help get that baby out of you, it will die. It will lose oxygen and die, and maybe so could you." The doctor lifted up and went to walk away.

Yet again, Secret refused to let the woman go. She pulled the doctor back down to her. With

a trembling lip and meaning every word tha
escaped her mouth, she said to the doctor, "The
let us die."

The doctor just stood there for a moment. Se
cret's words had penetrated her soul, splintere
her soul. She knew what she had to do as guil
instantaneously flooded her being. She hope
she wouldn't live to regret her decision. Sh
hoped her patient and her patient's unborn bab
wouldn't suffer from the results of her decision.